Joy & Hope

Ethan Dulane is a Character Created by Candy Cain & Nicole Mullaney for Joy & Hope.

Other books written by Nicole Mullaney include:

Ivy and Mistletoe
Magic in Mount Holly (coming soon)
The Maltese Holiday (coming soon)
Deck the Heart (coming soon)

For Adult Romance Check out Nikki A Lamers

<u>The Unforgettable Series:</u>
The Unforgettable Summer
Unforgettable Nights
Unforgettable Dreams
Unforgettable Memories
The Unforgettable One

<u>The Home Duet</u>:
Dreams Lost and Found
Finding Home

Joy & Hope

By Ethan Dulane

Table of Contents

Copyright

ISBN 978-1-951185-02-2 (paperback)
ISBN 978-1-951185-04-6 (e-book)

Cover design by Constantine Chutis
Image by Marisol Farrell

Dedication

To Allie and Catherine, our inspiration for Joy & Hope.

Chapter 1

Hope

I swiftly tack my horse, Westie, preparing him for a ride. I tighten the girth underneath him and adjust the stirrups. I finish and look up at him, lovingly stroking his dark brown neck and nearly black mane, the repetitive motion soothing for both of us. He's a beautiful Bay thoroughbred horse. He's twenty-two years old and fifth generation Secretariat. He's an absolutely incredible horse. He neighs, softly, nudging his nose towards me adoringly, bringing a smile to my lips. He has such a sweet disposition. It may sound strange to some people, but he's always been there for me and I'm grateful for it. I reach into my light blue jean jacket pocket and pull out a treat. I lay my hand flat and hold the treat out to Westie. He carefully grabs the treat out of my hand with his lips and flops it back into his mouth. I smile and brush my hands off as I continue to pet him.

I look around the ranch, enjoying the quiet of the early morning. My grandparents built Two Sisters Ranch back in the sixties and then my mom and dad eventually took over most of the every day work. So, I've lived here my whole life. This time of day, when the sun has just begun to shine and it's quiet except for the sounds of the wind in the trees and the animals moving around, it has always been one of my favorites. I'm surrounded by corrals, stables, and greens from all the trees filling the horse trails and I can't even come close to seeing it all, at least not with just standing here. The ranch covers about five-hundred acres of property. Of course, our house is on the property. Plus, we have The Inn at Two Sisters Ranch for people who want to come and stay with us and enjoy the benefits of living here for their vacation.

I personally enjoy spending most of my time taking care of the animals. Of course, we have several ranch hands, but I'd rather be with the horses. We have one hundred and one horses and so many of them are different breeds. Most of the horses belong to our family, but a few of the horses, like Casper have a different owner who pays to have us house and take care of them. Casper is a sleek, jet-black Draft horse and he's the only one we have here.

A loud rumbling sound pulls my attention towards the stables. I glance up, the dark brown wood of the buildings near me show a reddish tint in the sunlight. I watch as Gabe steps between the doors, causing my stomach to flip at the sight of him. He rolls both doors back, opening them all the way, one at a time. He's wearing a pair of dark blue work jeans, a navy blue, dark red and white flannel shirt, with his thick, brown, corduroy coat, hanging open over the top. I bite my lower lip and look away, letting my long brown hair fall over my face before he even has a chance to glance in my direction.

Gabe works here as the lead ranch hand, but he's also been my best friend my whole life. I can admit to myself, he also makes my heart beat out of control, but I don't know if I can actually tell him that or if I ever will. I'm afraid he doesn't feel the same and I don't ever want to lose him. His five feet ten inches feels as if he's towering over my petite five feet four inch frame, but I like that. He has wavy dark brown hair and bright green eyes. He's always watching out for me and going out of his way to help. His face has a diamond shape with an adorable dimple on his chin. Then when he smiles at me, it feels as if everything will be okay, even when they're not. I hear the familiar sound of his brown, work boots hitting the dirt as he approaches me. I glance up and my face immediately breaks out into a bright smile in welcome.

"Morning, Hope," he greets me, his voice raspy this morning. He gives me the same familiar smile I've known and loved my whole life, warming my insides.

"Hi, Gabe," I reply.

"I would have gotten Westie ready," he insists. He gestures to the horse standing patiently next to me.

"Oh, I finished mucking the stables early and I saw that Joy had a ride scheduled," I inform him. I recheck Westie's straps, trying not to look Gabe in the eyes. I know he's not happy I did all that work by myself, but I couldn't sleep and I had to keep myself busy.

"Need help?" he offers.

I give my head a shake. "Nah, I got it," I respond. I pat Westie adoringly on his side and croon, "Don't I Westie boy?"

Gabe grins and leans against the wooden wall of the stables, watching me. I feel my face heat with his eyes focused on me. I push my shoulders back, feigning confidence. I turn my head to look at him, challenging him with an arch of my eyebrows and I smile in question.

His grin broadens and he glances down at his feet. He pushes off the wall, his cheeks turning slightly pink. He clears his throat and glances at the clipboard in his hand. "You did all of the stables?" he clarifies, sounding surprised.

I nod my head in confirmation. "Yeah, well, all the stables on this side of the ranch. I got up at five. I couldn't sleep," I admit, shrugging like it's no big deal. "So, I figured I'd get it done," I explain.

"Seems like a pretty easy day," Gabe mutters. I know he's still staring at me, watching me for my reaction.

I nod my head in agreement. "Yeah, we've got a lot of people checking out," I remind him, attempting to maintain my focus on Westie. "Dad and Joy are going to take care of the rooms," I inform him.

"Does that mean you have the day off?" he questions, sounding happy at the prospect.

I laugh in response. I finally turn to really look at him, my big brown eyes meeting his gaze. I notice the corners of his mouth twitch up in amusement. "Gabriel, when do I ever have a day off?" I probe, my sarcasm clear.

He shrugs and chuckles softly, the sound giving me goosebumps. "Well, you can take one today, if you want. I can handle all this," he offers, warming me from the inside out. "If the inn is taken care of, you're good to go. Why don't you head into town?" he proposes.

My heart drops into the pit of my stomach and my head falls, instinctively, glancing down at my scuffed, dark brown cowboy boots. I grimace, forcing myself to get busy by grabbing treats for Westie. I hold my hand flat and offer him one. Without looking at Gabe, I softly murmur, "You know I like it better here, Gabe."

He heaves a heavy sigh, sounding defeated. "Yeah, I know," he concedes, sadly. I pinch my lips tightly together, my chest aching at his reaction. I wish I could do better for him, but I'm just not ready to leave the ranch. I just can't.

I take the tethers off of Westie as I grab onto his lead, guiding him out of the stable. I attempt to think of something that will help ease Gabe's mind. I don't want him to worry about me so much. "Tell you what," I begin,

11

"you go grab us lunch from town later today and we can both have a long lunch break," I suggest.

I glance at Gabe out of the corner of my eye, my heart skipping a beat at the broad smile that lights up his face. "Deal," he agrees.

I nod my head and quietly breathe a sigh of relief at his reaction. "See you later, Gabe," I murmur. Then, I turn and walk away, leading Westie.

"Bye," he calls after me.

I feel his eyes on me as I saunter off, causing me to feel a rush of warmth spread throughout my body. I take a deep breath, inhaling the fresh air. I look up, smiling at the sight of my younger sister, Joy riding Sport, an eighteen year old, chestnut, Irish Sport horse, around the corral. I slow my pace so I can watch her momentarily, her long, dark blond hair blowing in the wind behind her. She's wearing dark blue fitted jeans, dark brown cowboy boots and a thick, red and black checkered coat, lined with wool and folded down at her collar. Out of the two of us, to me, she's the one who always seems so stylish and well put together, while I wear what I think is cute, but most importantly, I have to be comfortable working in it. As she turns and circles back in my direction, I yell out to her, "Hey, Joy."

Her bright blue eyes, frame her long lashes and widen the moment she spots me. She immediately grins from ear to ear. "Hey, Hope! Thanks for getting Westie ready," she calls out, appreciatively.

"Are you going to ride him?" I inquire.

She stops and dismounts Sport before answering. "Yeah," she confirms. "He's too much horse for anyone else," she claims.

"Except me, of course," I remind her.

She arches her eyebrows in surprise before she agrees. "Yeah, if you ever rode off the ranch," she grumbles.

I ignore her comment and prompt, "So who is riding?"

"Joan Elkhart," she answers. "She and her husband are checking out today and she wanted to get one more ride in," she informs me.

"Alone?" I question, surprised.

Joy gives me a look, arching her eyebrows in challenge. "She's got me," she retorts, sarcastically.

I fight the urge to roll my eyes at her. "You know what I mean," I emphasize. "Where's her husband?" I inquire.

She shrugs as if she hadn't even thought of it, "I don't know. I didn't ask. I'll probably find out on the ride," she adds.

I grimace at her answer. "I hope they didn't get into a fight or anything," I murmur.

She shakes her head in denial, "No, he booked the trail ride for her."

I breathe a sigh of relief. Mr. and Mrs. Elkhart have been coming to the ranch for a very long time and I've always enjoyed them. I want them to be happy. "Oh, good," I mumble. "Where are you going?" I prod.

"Just around the lake and back," she reveals. "She doesn't do more than walk, so it will be a nice morning for her," she adds, thoughtfully.

"Pictures and such," I comment. We both know Mrs. Elkhart very well. Over the years, with them coming back every year, we've gotten to know them as so much more than guests. More than anything, she has always seemed to love taking pictures all over the ranch. Plus we've seen some of her pictures and they are truly incredible. She even blew one of them up for us and gave it to us as a gift in memory of our mom and aunt. Now, we have it hanging in one of our guest rooms.

Joy grins and nods in affirmation. "Exactly," she concurs.

"Stay away from Devil's Shelf," I advise.

"Why?" she probes.

"Gabe told me the wind and rain shifted the rocks last month," I inform her. I gulp over the lump in my throat, just thinking of how dangerous that could be.

"So?" she challenges.

My eyes widen in shock. "So there could be a rock slide," I blurt out, as my heart begins to beat erratically. "The last thing we need is for you to get hurt," I add. I feel a growing panic, but I concentrate on my breathing, attempting to keep it under control.

She rolls her eyes at me, dramatically and heaves a heavy sigh. "I'll be fine," she declares, defiantly.

"Joy!" I yell. My heart begins racing, pushing my blood so fast, I hear it pounding in my ears. My palms start to sweat and I glance down at my hands, already shaking. "Stay away from that trail," I demand. "It's not safe!" I reiterate, feeling desperate.

Joy swiftly dismounts Sport. She steps towards me and puts her hand up, as if waving a white flag of surrender in my direction. "Okay, okay," she relents, placating me. "I wasn't going that way to begin with," she admits. I breathe a sigh of relief, but narrow my eyes at her for taunting me. "I'm taking her around the lake and back. That's it," she emphasizes, knowing I need a little extra comfort after this conversation.

I take a deep breath, settling my nerves and nod my head in agreement. "I'm having lunch with Gabe, so don't be late, okay?" I request.

"Oh," she says, dragging out the word and teasing me. A playful grin lights up her face. "Gabriel, eh?" she prompts, wiggling her eyebrows.

I feel my heartbeat pick up its pace and my cheeks blush a deep shade of red. "Stop," I plead, a smile pulling at the corners of my mouth and trying to break through. "It's only lunch," I proclaim.

She grins even wider and gives me a knowing look. "Sure it is," she mumbles, playfully, appearing satisfied. She always insists Gabe and I should be together.

Out of the corner of my eye, I notice the straight, shoulder-length red hair of Mrs. Elkhart approaching us. I call out to her, needing a subject change. "Hi, Mrs. Elkhart! Joy is all ready for you!" I announce. She's wearing black pants, top and boots, with a thick, cardigan sweater over top in a design of various geometric shapes colored in red, orange, yellow, black and brown.

She waves at us as she approaches and we wave back. Joy leans a little closer to me and mumbles under her breath, "We'll finish this later."

I smile and shake my head at Joy, happy to be out of the conversation for now. I nod my head in greeting towards Mrs. Elkhart as she steps up to us, with a bright smile, ready for her ride. "Hi, Hope. Hi, Joy," she murmurs, in her soft voice. Her blue eyes, light up with excitement as she steps up to Westie, with her professional looking camera strapped around her neck.

"Hi, Mrs. Elkhart," Joy greets her. "Are you ready?" she inquires. She nods her head in confirmation. I make my way over to the gate to release it for them to head out to the trails, while I figure out what's next on my list.

Chapter 2

Ethan

I disconnect the call with my publisher's assistant, Beatrice and glance at the time. I better get going. She made it sound like it was urgent. I push back from my desk and gently close my laptop. I grimace, knowing I wasn't really getting anywhere with this book anyway. I stand and walk over to glance in the mirror. I need to make sure I'm at least put together for this last minute meeting with my publisher. I'm wearing black pants and a black thermal. It's perfect for working, but not for meeting Amanda. I quickly tug a charcoal button down dress shirt out of my closet and pull it on, grateful there don't appear to be any wrinkles. I button it up and tuck my shirt in, before I slip on my shiny, black, lace-up dress shoes. I lightly brush my hand over my short, dark brown, perfectly coifed hair, noticing my hazel eyes have a touch of gold today. I grab my keys, my wallet and my black leather jacket, throwing it on as I rush out the door of my New York City apartment.

I ride the elevator down to the small lobby area and soon step out onto the sidewalk. I turn left, striding past people of all ages going about their own business and heading in every direction. As I rush to Amanda's office, I can't help but wonder exactly what she wants from me. I believe I still have some time to finish this book. I grimace, hoping I'm right. I ignore the sounds of the people and traffic, while I attempt to come up with something to give her. I should at least give her some kind of progress, but I don't like what I have, especially since I keep starting over. How do I tell her that? I heave a sigh as I pull the heavy glass door open to her building. I walk inside and stride up to the tall, silver desk, immediately handing the security guard standing behind it my driver's license. The tall, older man with gray hair and broad shoulders, quickly checks me in, before he offers me a stiff nod and a welcoming smile. I step over to the elevator and press the up button. Only a moment later, the doors slide open and I step inside. I press the button for Amanda's floor and step towards the back as I ride the elevator up to her office.

I step off the elevator, slip my coat off and hang it on a hook in the wall to my left as soon as I walk into the front office of the publishing company. I step up to a long, black desk with "Parkington Publishing" written in bold, black letters on the wall behind the desk. I smile broadly, greeting Amanda's assistant, "Hi, Beatrice."

Beatrice is an older woman with a round face and short, gray, curled hair. She smiles wide as her kind brown eyes meet mine. "Ethan, you made it," she announces, sounding pleased.

I nod in acknowledgement. "I got here as quickly as I could," I murmur.

She nods in understanding and informs me, "Amanda said you could go right in the moment you arrive."

"Thank you," I politely mumble. I take a deep breath and exhale slowly to calm my nerves, before I step up to the large oak door with the golden nameplate, "Amanda Parkington," placed right at the top of the door. I knock twice on the door and peek inside. Amanda is sitting on one of her two blue and black tiger striped couches, reading a manuscript. She waves her hand for me to enter without even glancing up at me. I step inside her office and start to approach her. "Hi, Aman..." I trail off as she holds her finger up to stop me from speaking, still focused on the manuscript. I close my mouth and clasp my hands behind me, as I stand awkwardly looking around her office and waiting for her to finish.

This office definitely suits her. Amanda has flawless, soft brown skin, brown eyes, high cheekbones and short, straight black hair that angles down to her chin and goes up as it moves towards the back. She's wearing a dark teal leather skirt and a silk sleeveless top with matching pumps, accessorized with a long, gold and pearl necklace layered together, a gold watch and gold earrings. She's a beautiful woman at five feet seven inches. Plus, even in the way she holds herself, she has a powerful and intelligent vibe radiating off of her. Then again, she has a very well known publishing company. I was thrilled and appreciative when she offered me my first contract. She has been an incredible publisher for my other books. The last thing I want to do would be to disappoint her. I glance at her massive mahogany desk; the top clear except for her computer, phone, a container full of pens and what I assume is a short stack of manuscripts. Then, I turn and glance outside her window at the view of other unique, New York City skyscrapers.

Amanda straightens, the movement bringing my attention back to her. She places a bookmark in the manuscript before she sets it down on the small mahogany coffee table in front of her and looks up at me. "Ethan," she announces.

"Hi, Amanda. You wanted to see me?" I inquire, taking a step towards her.

She nods her head in confirmation. "Yes. Have a seat," she offers. She pats a spot on the opposite end of the couch she's sitting on.

I step in front of the couch and cautiously lower myself down next to her, anxious for what she has to say. "I came as soon as Beatrice called. She said it was urgent," I prompt.

"It is," she affirms. She purses her lips and leans back against the couch, assessing me. She folds her hands in front of her and tilts her head to the side, watching me, making me slightly uneasy. "Ethan," she begins, "how long ago did I publish your first book?" she questions.

I pause and quickly do the math in my head. Then, I look at her and murmur my response, "Uh, seven years."

"Seven years, three months and two days," Amanda amends, confidently.

I nod slowly and give a slight shrug, not sure why she's giving me such an exact number. "Okay," I murmur, dragging out the word. "You would know better than I would," I concede.

"And your second book?" she prods.

I pause, thinking for a moment. "Six," I reply.

"Five years, nine months and five days," she corrects, not leaving any room for argument. "Your third?" she prompts.

"Amanda, I'm really grateful to Parkington Publishing for releasing all five of my books over the past seven years and three months," I emphasize, not quite sure where she's going with this.

"And two days," she reminds me.

"Right," I grumble, suddenly even more on edge.

"You've had a book published every eighteen months with Parkington," she reiterates.

I nod my head slowly, while my knee begins bouncing nervously. Every statement that leaves her

19

mouth makes me a little more apprehensive. "About that, yes," I agree.

"You have a great deal of fans," she declares, boldly.

I feel my heartbeat speed up and my palms becoming increasingly sweaty with every moment Amanda seems to drag out this conversation. "Yes, yes I certainly do," I attest. I wouldn't be able to be doing what I love without my fans and I love writing.

"They love your romance adventure stories. All five of your books," she reiterates, as if she's bragging about my books or even about me, confusing me even more. "So, do you know what our little problem is?" she challenges, with an arch of her eyebrow.

I grimace, finally knowing where she's going with this. Then again, I think I knew what she wanted even before I walked through the door. I hesitantly concede, making it sound more like a question, "You want another book?"

She gives me a look, as if my comment is ridiculous and pushes to her feet. "No, I don't want another book, Ethan. Your fans want the book," she emphasizes, looking down at me. She spins on her heel and begins pacing her office as she talks. "They've been waiting and it's been nearly eighteen months," she reminds me. "I don't want another book," she repeats. "I need another book," she declares, emphatically.

"I'm working on it," I insist.

She stops pacing and spins around, staring down at me. "Are you?" she prompts, her disbelief obvious. "Are you really, Ethan?" she reiterates. "Because I want another book for Valentine's Day and I haven't even gotten a rough draft from you yet," she informs me, of what we both already know and something I don't.

My eyes widen and my mouth drops open in shock. "Valentine's Day?" I gasp. "That's only two months from now!" I exclaim.

She grimaces and placates me. "I know dear. But that's eighteen months. And your contract says that you would give me six books by Valentine's Day. That will be nine years that I personally signed you," she reminds me.

"But, two months to write a novel?" I question, my eyes as wide as saucers.

She shakes her head and lowers herself back onto the couch next to me. She looks at me without apology and proclaims, "No, dear."

My hand goes to my chest as I breathe a sigh of relief. "Oh, thank goodness," I murmur, momentarily feeling better. Unfortunately, my relief doesn't last long.

"Two months, one week and four days to release a novel," she clarifies, giving a firm nod of her head for emphasis.

My mouth drops open in astonishment. "You can't be serious!" I grumble.

"Ethan, if I had a sense of humor, I wouldn't joke about this," she asserts. "You've got writer's block," she surmises.

I flinch and shift uncomfortably in my seat. I know it's true, but I hate to admit it. I keep writing I'm just not finding a good direction for any story and then I toss it and start over. I don't like anything I've written lately. "No, I've just done it all before," I claim. "Love at sea, love in the mountains, love at the beach, love in the country, love in the city..." I trail off as I think about what comes next, but my mind is blank.

"Love at a ranch," she adds to my list.

My eyebrows draw down in confusion. "I never wrote anything at a ranch," I proclaim. Maybe she has me mixed up with another one of her authors.

Amanda reaches over to the coffee table and picks up a colorful brochure of a horse ranch. She holds it out to me with a pleased smile. I cautiously take it from her, wondering what she'll say next. I glance at the cover of the brochure, displayed with two young girls riding horses. "But you will," she declares.

"What's this?" I inquire.

I open it, still debating why she's giving this to me. I know nothing about a ranch or ranch life for that matter. There's no way I can write a book in that setting. And besides, it's not exactly a good time for a vacation. I leaf through it as I listen to her explanation. "A little bit of inspiration for you. I took the liberty of booking you a two week stay at Two Sisters Ranch in Evergreen Valley in upstate New York," she announces, proudly.

I groan reflexively, at the realization of what she wants me to do. "Upstate? How far?" I question.

She shrugs as if the details don't matter. "Far enough to get you out of Manhattan and bring you some inspiration for you to write your next best seller," she proclaims, grinning.

"When do I leave?" I probe, in resignation.

"Today," she enlightens me and stands back up.

My eyes widen in surprise. "Today? I still need to pack!" I declare.

"Well, your train is in three hours," she enlightens me. "You'd better hurry," she prods. "Beatrice has all of your travel documents," she updates me.

I try to think about anything I may have coming up in my calendar in the next two weeks. It is December after all and with the holidays only a few weeks away, I have a lot of things to do. "What about Christmas?" I question.

"You'll be back on December twenty-third," she informs me.

I stand up with the brochure in my hand, as I frantically begin running through everything I need to do in the next couple hours to make it to the train in time. I offer Amanda a forced smile. I sarcastically grumble, "Thanks."

She smiles broadly, her eyes bright. "You can thank me in your book," she suggests. "Close the door on your way out," she requests.

I open my mouth to say something else to Amanda to stop this, but I stop myself as she turns back to her manuscript and picks it up. She removes the bookmark and returns to reading where she left off. I snap my mouth closed and turn away, knowing there's no point in arguing. I quickly stride for the door. I shake my head in disbelief as I pull her door shut behind me. I stop at Beatrice's desk and she hands me a large manila envelope with all the information I need for the trip along with a look of empathy. "Thanks," I mumble, sincerely. "I'll look it over on the train," I reveal.

"I emailed you all the documents as well," she advises. I force an appreciative smile. "Good luck, Ethan," she kindly offers. Then, she waves as I turn and quickly stalk towards the door.

"Thanks!" I reiterate, calling over my shoulder, just before the door swings shut behind me. I groan and run my hand through my hair in frustration. "I need someone to watch King," I mumble to myself. I grab my phone and pull up my cousin Denise's contact. I tap her phone number knowing I have to try her before I step into the elevator and wait for the call to connect, hoping she's going to be around the next few weeks.

She picks up after the first ring. "Hey, Ethan!" she greets me cheerfully.

I heave a sigh, desperate for her help. "Hi Denise. Are you around the next couple weeks?" I ask her, getting right to the point.

"Yeah," she states. "Why?"

"Is there any way you can pack an overnight bag and meet me at my place in the next thirty minutes?" I request. "I really need your help," I emphasize.

"What's going on?" she questions. "Is everything okay?" she prompts, sounding slightly panicked.

"Everything's fine," I insist, immediately calming her anxiety. "I just need to leave for work for a couple weeks," I add.

"What?" she prompts.

I heave a sigh and repeat, "Just come over. I have to get home and pack. I'll explain when you get to my place."

"Okay, no problem," she instantly agrees.

"Great!" I proclaim and breathe a sigh of relief. "I'll see you soon," I mumble. I tap end to disconnect the call, just as I step onto the elevator and push the button for the lobby. I sigh heavily as the doors close, anxiously waiting for them to reopen at the ground level and I'm able to rush home. I don't have time to think about this until I'm on that train.

Chapter 3

Ethan

I close one more button on my navy blue dress shirt, leaving the top by my collar open. I grab the small, navy travel bag with all my bathroom items, pausing to make sure I have everything. Then, I swing the door open and step into my bedroom. I have a small one-bedroom apartment, but at least I have a decent sized bedroom for living in the city. I feel fortunate to have an extra half bath in the main living area between the kitchen and living room, which is really one room, but an extra anything is something unheard of around here. My view of a red brick wall has something to be desired, but a little extra space is worth it to me.

I pull another navy suitcase out from my closet and toss it on the bottom of my bed, on top of my gray comforter, quickly zipping it open. I flip the top back and then I step over to the wire rack in the corner of my bedroom. I glance at the stacks of clothes piled up to the ceiling. I don't really have time to go through everything right now. I'll just have to pack extra to make sure I have all that I need, although I'm not really sure what I'm going to need on a ranch. I reach for a tall stack of shirts and sweaters, picking up the whole pile. I spin on my heel, turning towards my bed and take the two paces to close the distance. I place the whole pile neatly inside and then spin around, repeating the process with another stack of clothes.

"Let me get this straight," my cousin, Denise begins. I glance down at her, as she looks at me with wide eyes. She has shoulder length blonde hair, pale skin, blue-grey eyes and she's about four inches shorter than me. The only features we seem to share would be the oval shape of our face and what we call the Dulane family smile. I'm thankful she lives so close and she was able to get here so quickly to help me out. "Your boss is making you go to a ranch for two weeks, so you can write another book," she reiterates. She lowers herself down onto the corner of my bed by the pillows, waiting for my response. My cat, King, immediately climbs into her lap, pushing his head into her black shirt and tan and black large-checkered cardigan. He usually doesn't love much attention, but for some reason he craves it from my cousin. King is an orange Maine Coon cat, with a very large appetite and a round belly to show for it. She smiles down at King and begins mindlessly petting him. He purrs and happily settles next to her on the bed.

I smile in spite of my current situation and nod my head in confirmation. "Yes," I reaffirm.

She glances up at me and grins. "You know, you've got a pretty cool job, Ethan," she announces, sounding impressed.

I huff a laugh of disbelief. "Yeah, right," I mutter, sarcastically. "I get blindsided with an exile upstate under the threat of not having a job if I don't write a book," I grumble, irritably. I grit my teeth as I continue moving between the shelves and my suitcase, packing. I guess I could always search for another publisher, but you need a book to be able to do that and I obviously don't have one right now. Plus, leaving without fulfilling my contract would look bad for anyone. It doesn't matter how much you've produced prior or how well you've done. No one would want to take me on. I'd be too much of a risk.

She freezes and gasps as her mouth drops open in shock at my response. "Your job's at stake?" she probes, with obvious disbelief.

I flinch just hearing the words out loud. "Yes. No," I stammer. I heave a sigh and run my hand down my face in exasperation. "I don't know," I finally concede. "Don't say anything to my mom, okay?" I request, desperately.

She straightens and puts her hands up, as if in surrender. "I won't," she claims. "My lips are sealed," she adds. She pretends to zip her lips shut and throw away the key, before she continues petting King. "I'm sure you'll come back with your next best seller," she proclaims, with the same confidence I wish I could take along with me.

I stop packing and assess her. She looks like she believes her statement. I just hope she's right. "Do you really think so?" I prod.

She gives me an encouraging smile. "I know so," she confirms. "You've always been the creative one in the family, Ethan," she praises. "Besides," she shrugs, "you work really great under pressure," she reminds me.

I nod slowly in acknowledgement, grateful for her assessment. "True," I mumble, a small smirk touching my lips. But she's right. When I know I have a deadline coming up, I don't have any choice, but to focus. There's no reason this book will be any different. I just need a really good idea to run with. I heave a sigh. Maybe spending time at a ranch upstate is just what I need. I definitely need to do something drastic to be able to push my personal feelings aside and find the happily ever after I need for my book.

"A couple of weeks out of the city will probably do you some good," she reiterates, as if it's a known fact.

That's exactly what Amanda seems to believe too. "I hope you're right," I murmur, as I reach for more clothes.

I feel Denise's questioning gaze focused on me. I brace myself, anticipating her next question. She finally opens her mouth, hesitating another moment before she inquires, "Could you really lose your job if you don't write a book in two weeks?"

I wince and exhale slowly before I answer. "No, it's not really like that. I'm a freelance writer. Parkington is my publisher. I'm supposed to give them more books than I have and they're getting antsy," I explain, in attempt to keep it simple.

She nods in understanding. Then she looks up at me and grins. "Well, your fans are getting antsy too," she claims.

"Come on, Denise," I grumble. I shake my head brushing off her comment. I walk over to my simple oak rectangular desk with a matching chair. I reach for my laptop, cords, extra flash drives, pens and papers I might need, including the ones Beatrice handed to me earlier and then I slip everything inside my black briefcase. I flip the top flap of my briefcase back over the top and clamp it shut.

She shrugs as if she's heard it one hundred times before. Then she exclaims, "I'm serious, Ethan! All of my friends keep asking me when my cousin, the famous author, is releasing his next book," she explains, with a dramatic flair.

I smirk, showing my amusement with her antics; at the same time I shake my head in disbelief. "I'm hardly famous," I mumble, with a small shrug of my shoulders. I realize people read my books or I wouldn't be where I am today, but it's about the books and the stories, not about me. I'm just me.

She arches her eyebrows in challenge. "You're famous enough that people want to read your work," she reminds me.

I pinch my lips tightly together and exhale slowly at her words. I murmur under my breath, so she can't hear me, "I hope so." I love to write and tell stories, especially ones filled with romance and adventure. Having other people read them and enjoy them is a bonus and an honor. Then again, I wouldn't be able to write books for a living if people didn't read them. I glance at my watch, attempting to forget about her statement and focus on what I need to do now. "Alright, I really gotta' go if I'm going to catch this train," I inform her. I pause and look her in the eyes and question one last time, "Are you sure you don't mind staying here and taking care of King?"

"Not at all," she states, waving away my worry as she pets him. "It will be a nice break from Brooklyn," she claims.

I nod my head and give her another grateful smile. "Well, help yourself to anything," I offer. "Okay?" I prod.

She nods in agreement and grins, "I will."

"This trip is so last minute," I mumble, the obvious. "What I mean is, I wasn't planning on going anywhere, so I just went grocery shopping. There's tons of food in the refrigerator. I don't want it to go to waste," I emphasize.

"Thanks," she responds, appreciatively.

"And if there are any problems, I'll have my cell and laptop," I reiterate. I run over everything I've already told her in my head, trying to decide if I shared everything she needs to know while I'm away.

She smirks and teases, "If you actually get Wi-Fi up there."

The corners of my mouth twitch up in amusement. "Ha-ha, very funny," I mumble, sarcastically. Then again, she might be right. I sigh softly and give a slight shake of my head, hoping for the best. What else can I do?

"Have a good time," she encourages, sweetly.

I grimace as I zip up my suitcase. "Yeah, right," I groan. I grab my black leather coat off the post of my wire rack and slip it on. Then, I step towards Denise. She stands up and I wrap my arms around her in an appreciative hug. She gives me a light squeeze in return before I release her. "See you in two weeks," I declare.

She grins and proclaims, "I'll be here!"

"Thanks," I emphasize, again. She nods her head in acknowledgement. I heave another sigh and do one last quick glance around my room, hoping I didn't forget anything I might need.

Denise glances down at King and begins talking in a high-pitched voice, "We'll be here! Yes, we will," she murmurs. She lowers her voice and continues having a conversation with my cat, "Bye, Daddy. Yeah, you and me."

I chuckle as I gather my things. I pick my suitcase up off the bed and pull the handle up. I grab my black hanging bag and slip the hanger through the handle of my suitcase. I sling my briefcase over my shoulder and my bathroom bag over my other shoulder. Then I grab my other matching suitcase and pull the handle up. I awkwardly stalk out my door and make my way towards the elevator at the end of the hall. I can't help but feel slightly overloaded, but I didn't want to forget anything when I'm going to be there for so long. I set my suitcases down and glance at my watch one more time to verify I'm still on schedule to make the train. I breathe a sigh of relief as the elevator doors slide open in front of me. I grasp all my things and clumsily stumble onto the elevator with a groan. I let go of one suitcase to tap the button for the first floor and wait impatiently until the doors reopen.

I stride through our small lobby and step outside into the crisp, winter air, my breath instantly becoming visible. I immediately step towards the curb, holding up my arm trying to hail a cab. I know there's no way I'll make it to the train on time if I attempt to haul all this stuff down the sidewalk or even on the subway for that matter.

A cab pulls up to the curb in front of me. The driver opens the trunk and I quickly put all my things inside, before jumping in the back seat. "Penn Station near 8th and 33rd," I inform him. I sit back against the black, leather seats and buckle my seatbelt. I'm thankful traffic is light, making the drive short. In just a few minutes, we pull into Penn Station, located below Madison Square Garden. I pull out my wallet and the money for the fare, plus a generous tip. I quickly pay the cab driver through the small open slot in the thick plastic barrier between the driver and its passengers. Then, I hop out and make my way around the back of the cab. I grab all of my things out of the trunk, before I slam it closed.

I make my way down the escalator and pass by the strips of small shops and restaurants, before I stop at a large open area, leading to all different terminals, including Amtrak. I approach the electronic boards near the Amtrak designated waiting area to find where I need to go to catch my train. I spot my destination on the board just as the track number lights up. I swiftly make my way over to the track entrance. I stride down to the train platform before I briefly set one of my bags down to check the time. I glance at my watch and breathe a sigh of relief, realizing I've made it with only a few minutes to spare.

I readjust and grasp all my things again, just as the silver train with the familiar red and blue stripes pulls into the station and comes to a stop in front of me and several other passengers. The doors slide open and I haul myself through the doors. I quickly find my way to an empty row and lift my suitcases up, placing them on the metal racks above the seats. I pull the rest of my things into the seat with me and lower myself onto the navy blue, plastic, leather seat next to the window. I put my things on the empty seat beside me, the moment I realize the train is relatively vacant.

After getting myself settled on the train, I pull the paperwork Beatrice gave me out of my briefcase. "Looks like I'll be on this train for a few hours," I grumble to myself. I guess that will give me time to find out a little more about where I'm headed. I flip through the colorful brochure of Two Sisters Ranch. This place looks massive and incredibly beautiful. I sigh, looking at all the pictures of people riding horses through different parts of the ranch. I know absolutely nothing about horses. "This should be interesting," I mumble under my breath. I'm going to have to jump right into my research if I want this book to be any good.

My stomach growls, reminding me I didn't have time to eat anything. I reach into my bag, knowing I usually keep something in there just in case. I pull out a bag of potato chips and sigh. "It's better than nothing," I grumble to myself. I open the bag, crinkling the paper as I reach my hand in and pull a few out. I pop the first one in my mouth with a satisfying crunch. I sit back in my seat and stare out the window, while I eat. The tall buildings and endless concrete are soon replaced with more and more trees, until I see nothing but the blur of green,

brown underneath nearly cloudless blue skies outside my
window.

Chapter 4

Gabe

I dust my hands off on my jeans as I approach Two Sisters Inn. The inn itself is a large, white, 3-story, Victorian style home with an expansive wrap-around front porch and black shutters. Green garland with white lights wraps around the poles and railings of the front porch, accented with large, red, velvet bows, showcasing the start of our Christmas decorations. White rocking chairs line one side of the front door and small iron bistro tables with matching chairs line the other, scattered along the gray painted, wooden floorboards of the porch, overlooking the entrance to the ranch. I'm careful of the large, Christmas wreath, adorned with red berries and a big, red velvet bow, as I push the heavy, black front door in and step into the foyer, pulling the door closed behind me.

Stairs leading up to most of the guest rooms are directly in front of me, with a small hallway to a few more guest rooms behind the stairs to the right. I glance to my left, finding the front room nearly empty, except for the barn wood armoire in the corner and a couple pine accent tables, ready for more decorations. I look to my right, into the front office and immediately spot Frank McGregor, Joy and Hope's dad. Frank is a big man at six feet four inches, with a broad build and the biggest heart. He's bald on top with short, salt and pepper hair towards the back as well as in his neatly trimmed beard and mustache. He's wearing faded jeans, a cream and tan flannel shirt with staggered red stripes down and a faded red thermal underneath. He has the sleeves of his shirt rolled up, while he sits at a smaller desk behind the front desk, going through the ledger. He glances up from behind his dark brown-rimmed glasses as I greet him with a smile, "Hey, Mr. McGregor!"

"Hi, Gabe," he replies. "Need something?" he questions.

I shake my head in answer and announce, "No, Sir. I'm heading to Shandy's to pick up lunch for me and Hope," I enlighten him. "Would you like something?" I offer.

He shakes his head and tells me, "No thanks, Son. I just had a sandwich." I smile to myself at the endearment. I've known him my whole life and he has always treated me as part of the family. I have an amazing family of my own, but this ranch has always been like a second home to me, just like the McGregor's have been a second family to me.

"Okay," I acknowledge, with a firm nod. Then I turn around to leave.

Frank calls out, stopping me in my tracks. "Say, Gabe?" he prompts.

I spin back around and face him. "Yes Sir?" I inquire.

He sets the pen in his hand down and stands up. He saunters over to the front desk, placing his palms flat on the surface and leaning towards me. He looks me in the eyes and suggests, "Why don't you try to get Hope to go with you?"

I grimace and reveal, "I did. She wants to stay here. Said that there's a last minute guest coming that she wants to take care of."

He sighs heavily and I watch the disappointment wash over his features, making my own stomach churn. I want her to be ready just as much as everyone, maybe even more, but I want her to do it on her time. In the meantime, I'll just keep doing everything I can to support her, encourage her and be there for her. "Thanks for trying," he murmurs, forcing a small smile.

"Yeah," I mumble, pasting a tight smile on my face. "She'll go when she's ready," I insist, believing my words to be true. He nods his head, sadly and trudges back to the smaller desk, returning to his books. I turn around and walk out of the office, without another word. I step outside and pull the door closed behind me. I stride around the corner and make my way right to my old, blue pick-up truck.

I pull the door open and climb up onto the tan, cloth bench seat, behind the wheel of my truck. I turn the key and buckle my seatbelt before I reach up to put it in gear. I cautiously back out of the dirt driveway, until I can pull around the circle in front of the inn. I drive past the white post in front, with the hanging dark green wooden sign, carved and painted with gold lettering announcing, "The Two Sisters Ranch, est. 1968," before I pull out onto the old paved highway.

Like always, my thoughts immediately drift to Hope and her beautiful smile. I'd do anything to see her smile more like she used to, without the touch of sadness in her gorgeous brown eyes. When we were little kids, I'd play with both Joy and Hope all the time. I think I was in love with her even back then. We would have so much fun together, playing hide and seek in the barn, tag in the field, or just taking care of or riding the horses. It was rare to find Hope without a smile on her face or laughter in her voice. She was just always happy. I miss that sparkle in her eyes. I see a glimpse of it now and then.

I've made a promise to myself to keep trying to bring it back, to bring her back and I'm not going to stop until I do.

I don't blame her for having such a hard time. She's been through so much. It's been hard on everyone, but there's no doubt in my mind that Hope has had it the hardest. That fact makes my whole body ache, feeling her pain, as if it were my own. All I want to do is be there for her through it all, as long as she'll let me. I smile to myself, thinking about what to get her for lunch and knowing nothing has changed. I would still do absolutely anything to protect her, help her and make her happy. Hopefully, one day soon she'll realize it too. I know I couldn't imagine my life without her.

I pull into town and stop just before the light at the four corners. I park my truck along the side of the road, right on our picturesque Main Street. A lot of the shop owners are outside taking advantage of the weather while they still can and decorating the front of their shops for the holidays. We have a bank, a grocery store, a garage, a hardware and feed store, a pharmacy, a general store, a salon, a small clothing store, and a restaurant on each of the four corners in the center of town. The church, school, library, post office and all the emergency services buildings are just outside of town. I honestly don't think Evergreen Valley can be described as anything but quaint. I glance at Shandy's and grimace at the line already forming outside the front door. I glance over at the new café, remembering they finally opened. "Well, I guess it's time to check it out," I mumble to myself. I open the door and hop out of my truck, slamming the door behind me. I stop and look both ways, unsurprisingly finding no traffic in either direction. I jog across the street, making my way there.

Hope

I use one of the master keys to open the door and slip into the guest bedroom that we're turning over for the last minute guest arriving tonight. I walk into the room with a pine wreath looped through my arm, decorated with red holly berries and a thick red bow. I look around the bright and cheery room and smile to myself, noticing the room isn't ready yet. I know Joy and dad said they would get the guest rooms ready, but I can't sit still, so I'm grateful it's not done yet. Working keeps my mind focused on the task, instead of thinking too much. It works for me.

I set the wreath down on the stripped bed and step into the hallway. I stride to the closet and grab the vacuum, bringing it into the room. I slip off my shoes and step up onto the bed in my socks to center the wreath above the headboard. Then, I slide off the bed and put my shoes back on before I swiftly run a vacuum over the wood floors. I shake out the clean, white sheets, folded neatly on the mattress. Then, I walk around the bed, putting them on. I pull them tight and neatly fold down the top, before I add the simple gray patterned quilt. I straighten it out and add a white blanket, folding it neatly at the bottom of the bed in case the guest wants to use it. Then, I move to put the pillowcases on. I fluff the white, king-sized pillows before I place them tidily at the head of the bed. I hear the sound of boots tapping against the hardwood floors as someone walks into the room, bringing my gaze towards the entryway, just as Joy takes a step inside. I instinctively glance down at her feet and immediately notice her muddy cowboy boots. I gasp at the sight and my eyes widen in panic.

"I thought I'd find you in here," she mumbles, the moment she spots me. The corners of her mouth twitch up in amusement at seeing me doing some of her work.

"Joy! Out!" I demand, without preamble. "You're tracking mud everywhere. I just vacuumed!" I inform her, irritably.

She grimaces and then shrugs like it's no big deal. "Ah, I'll vacuum again," she announces, in attempt to reassure me. I narrow my eyes and scowl at her. At the same time, I pinch my lips tightly together to hold back my retort, knowing it won't do any good. "So, who is this new guest?" she inquires.

I sigh and go back to straightening the quilt, wanting to make it perfect. "I don't know," I answer. "He's not here yet."

"Dad said his train arrives at seven," she informs me. She walks to the opposite side of the bed and tries to help with the bed.

I nod in confirmation and then reach out to straighten one of the pillows. "Someone needs to get him from the station," I state.

"Why don't you do it?" she suggests. "It's not far," she claims. Then, she glances up at me in encouragement.

I look back at the bed, avoiding her gaze, as I gulp down the sudden lump in my throat. "I'll be cleaning up after dinner," I remind her.

"I can do that," she offers. "This gives you a reason to get off the ranch. You're going on ranch business," she proclaims.

I shake my head in refusal, not even taking a moment to think about it. "No, I'll stay here," I assert. Maybe if I don't leave any room for argument, she won't try to push me again. Unfortunately, I'm not so lucky.

"You should get out," she insists, casually, as if it's no big deal. I know she's trying to keep the conversation

39

light, but it feels like she's attempting to push me into the deep end and do something I don't want to do.

I cross my arms defiantly over my chest and turn my head towards Joy, glaring at her. "And you should mind your own business," I snap. Then, I throw the last pillow onto the bed, with more force than necessary.

Joy sighs in defeat and her hopeful gaze instantly turns apologetic. "I'm sorry, Hope. I just thought," she begins.

I immediately interrupt, not giving her a chance to explain. "Yeah, I know what you thought," I grumble. "And I know what everyone else thinks," I admit. I close my eyes and take a deep breath and exhale slowly, followed by another, attempting to calm my anxiety.

She bites her lower lip in thought. The room remains momentarily quiet and I feel her eyes lingering on me. "I'll pick him up," she finally concedes.

I exhale a sigh of relief and open my eyes to look at my sister. "Thank you," I mumble, appreciatively.

She pinches her lips tightly together and gives me a firm nod in acknowledgement, before she spins around to leave. Suddenly, she pauses in the doorway and spins back around to look at me. "You can't stay here forever, you know," she emphasizes.

I wince, tearing my gaze away from hers. I immediately go back to cleaning and straightening everything for the new guest, ignoring her words the best I can. Joy sighs heavily and leaves the room without another word. I force myself to keep moving until I hear her footsteps receding down the short hallway and the guest room door, opening and clicking closed behind her.

I exhale harshly and sit down on the edge of the bed I just finished making. I wish they would all stop pushing me so much. I know they're right, all of them. I should try to leave the ranch. I know Gabe and my family only want what's best for me. I realize staying here for as long as I have isn't normal, but what happened isn't normal either. What I saw wasn't normal. Can't they understand that? I'm the one who was there. I'm the one who saw it happen. I momentarily drop my head into my shaking hands, with my heart hammering inside my chest. I want to leave the ranch, especially for dad, Joy and Gabe, but I'm just not ready. Not yet. I drop my hands into my lap and take a few controlled, deep breaths, in and out. Then, I get up from the bed, push my shoulders back and stand tall, feigning confidence and strength I don't really feel.

I stride around the bed and straighten it out all over again, attempting to make it perfect. I need to finish up in here, so I can have this room prepared for the new guest before Joy comes back with him. Plus, Gabe should be back soon with our lunch and I want to run back out to the stables to check on the horses before we eat. I pull out my phone and glance at the time. If I hurry, I should have just enough time.

Chapter 5

Gabe

I stride around to the back of the inn, where I find a small iron bistro table with two matching chairs. I set it up a long time ago. We wanted a place to sit back here in the grass, just outside one of the stables, which is also where I'm sure to find Hope. I set the paper bag down, packed with our lunch. I look around, but I don't see Hope anywhere. She's almost always at the stable or close by at lunchtime. Plus, she knew I was coming. I turn around and call out for her, in the direction of the stables. "Hope, lunch!" I announce, loudly.

I open the bag, but pause as I hear the shuffle of footsteps, pulling my gaze upwards. My heart skips a beat at the sight of Hope walking out of the stables, squeezing hand sanitizer into her hands. She slips the small bottle into her coat pocket and begins rubbing her hands together. I clear my throat and force myself to look down, focusing on unpacking the food as she approaches. I pull out two sandwiches, an apple, a fruit cup and two small bags of potato chips. I lower myself into one of the chairs, just as she approaches and sits down across from me.

"What did you get?" she prompts.

I look up at her and smile in greeting. "I was going to get Shandy's, but there was a line, so I stopped at the new café in town," I reveal.

Her eyes widen and she arches her eyebrows in surprise. She questions, "There's a new café in town?"

I nod my head in confirmation. "Yeah, it opened yesterday. Mulberry Street Café," I enlighten her.

She smirks. "Let me guess," she prods and pauses. She looks up at me from underneath her long lashes and guesses, "It's on Mulberry Street?"

I nod in confirmation and grin over at her in amusement. "Good guess," I confirm. "Right on the corner of Mulberry and Main," I add, for her benefit. I want her to be able to picture where things are even if she isn't ready to leave with me, yet.

I hold out a turkey and cheese sandwich to Hope. She takes it from me, her hand lightly brushing mine in the exchange, causing chills to shoot up my arm and down my spine. She gives me a smile that only she can provide. It's the kind of smile that makes my heart skip a beat every single time it lights up her face. "Thank you," she mumbles, gratefully.

I gulp down the lump in my throat, before I respond. "You're welcome," I murmur. I glance up at her, suddenly anxious with anticipation. I would love to take her to the new café or anywhere really. I imagine taking her somewhere off the ranch, just the two of us, on a date, but I don't want to push her for something she's not ready to do either. I glance down at the food in front of me and then back at her, trying not to let my nerves get the best of me. I clear my throat and finally propose, "Maybe I can take you there for dinner this weekend?"

I bite the inside of my cheek and hold my breath, watching her intently for her reaction. She gasps and her eyes widen. She hesitates, obviously not knowing what to say. She takes a bite of her sandwich, as I wait for her reply, my heart lodged all the way up in my throat. She chews slowly, as if processing my words and then closes her eyes briefly in appreciation. Her eyes flutter open and she glances down at her sandwich. "Mm. Really good," she mumbles around her food.

I heave a sigh, as my heart drops to my gut and disappointment washes over me, yet again. I want to spend time with her away from here, just us. I want to take her on dates and show her how special she is to me. I want her to be mine and me to be hers and I want to share it with the world. But how can I when I can't even get her to spend time with me away from here? I pick up my own turkey sandwich and glance at her, my heart heavy. Will she ever give me a chance? "You can't hide out on the ranch forever, Hope," I grumble.

She visibly flinches, making me wince. Then, she instantly straightens her shoulders, putting her shields up and protecting herself from me, causing me to feel like she punched me in the stomach. "I'm not hiding out," she protests, defiantly.

"Hope," I plead, but she refuses to meet my gaze. "Hope!" I repeat her name, louder, feeling a little desperate.

She looks up at me through narrowed eyes and quietly snaps, "What?"

I've said this much, I might as well keep going. "This isn't healthy," I remind her, sadly.

She glares across the table at me, through narrowed eyes. "You sound like my dad," she grumbles, irritably.

I recoil at her comment, but I force myself to keep going, needing her to understand. I have to do something to really help her, instead of just being there for her and then staying quiet while she continues to ignore her feelings and keep herself so busy she doesn't even have time to process anything, let alone grieve or move on. The way she's been handling things is obviously not working for her or anyone else for that matter. It's time to try something different. I take a deep breath, steeling myself, preparing for her reaction. "You're pushing five years not leaving the ranch, Hope," I emphasize, attempting to get her to grasp how worried we all are about her. "People are," I begin and trail off, not able to find the right words. She interrupts me before I have the chance.

"People are what?" she prompts, arching her eyebrows in challenge. "Talking about me?" she probes, testily.

"No," I reply, automatically. I instantly give her a firm shake of my head. "They're worried about you," I contend.

She huffs a humorless laugh as she shakes her own head in response. "Like who?" she questions, her disbelief clear in her tone.

"Your dad. Joy," I respond, giving her the obvious answers first. I pause and take another deep breath, trying to calm my nerves. My heart clenches tightly in my chest and I exhale slowly. I hold her gaze, needing her to know how much it matters to me, how much *she* matters to me. I softly, but confidently declare, "Me."

She picks up her sandwich and stares at it momentarily. I hold my breath, desperately wanting to know what she's thinking. She keeps her eyes on her food, as she quietly responds, "There's no reason to be worried about me."

I close my eyes and exhale slowly, wishing that were true. Then, I reopen my eyes, with Hope my only focus. "Hope," I begin, her name a plea on the tip of my tongue.

She shakes her head vehemently, interrupting me before I continue. Her pain is written all over her face, instantly making me feel as if she knocked the wind out of me. "You weren't there, Gabe," she accuses, appearing completely vulnerable. She gives a sad shake of her head, as if she's trying to get rid of the images running through her mind from that night, causing my heart to break even more for her. I wish I were there that night, if only to protect her from the pain of what she saw. "I was," she rasps the reminder, her voice cracking with her agony, as she fights to hold back tears.

I grind my teeth together and gulp down the growing lump in my throat. "I know," I acknowledge. I hate the truth, but it doesn't matter. I'm not able to do anything about it and that physically hurts. "But staying here isn't going to bring them back," I remind her, making one more attempt to rationalize with her.

Her eyes flash with anger and she glares at me. My stomach flips at the look on her face, as I realize a little too late I said exactly the wrong thing. "I never said it would. I just feel safe here, okay?" she claims, enlightening me. I sigh heavily as my heart sinks into the pit of my stomach. That's why she doesn't ever want to leave? Her comment only makes me want to be there for her even more. I want to be the one to assist her in getting to a place in her life where she feels safe again. She can't stop living her life here or outside the ranch because of the past. She deserves to have the whole world handed to her and I want to be the one to do it, if she'll let me. "Just drop it," she requests, with an overwhelming sense of sadness in her soft brown eyes.

We both take a few bites of our sandwiches in silence. She stares out at the ranch, looking lost, while I can't take my eyes off of her. I hope I didn't push her too far. I just want what's best for her. I take a deep breath to calm my own anxiety. Then, I glance over at her, longing to turn this lunch with her around. It's definitely time to change the subject.

"Did you get the room ready for the new guest?" I inquire. She may have said earlier that her dad and Joy had it, but knowing Hope, she's the one who did the work, before they even had a chance to take a look inside the room.

She nods her head slowly and finally brings her attention back to me. I quietly breathe a sigh of relief as her beautiful, warm, brown eyes meet my green ones. "Yeah," she confirms, satisfied with my subject change. "He'll be here around seven or so. Joy's picking him up from the train station," she enlightens me.

I nod my head in both acknowledgement and understanding. "That's nice of her," I express, simply.

She nods her head in agreement and takes another bite of her sandwich. The light breeze blows her long brown hair around her shoulders as she chews, urging me to reach out and tuck it behind her ears, but I don't. "I want to start decorating for the tree lighting," she broadcasts. She looks at me with a hopeful expression and a small smile pulling at the corners of her mouth.

I know decorating for the tree lighting is something we have to do, but the tree hasn't even been delivered yet. I can't help but feel this came from out of nowhere, but the look on her face tells me it doesn't matter, as a small spark of something lights up her soft, brown eyes. I grin across the table at her. "I can't believe everyone will be here this Sunday to help decorate the tree already! It came so quick," I concede, in realization.

Her smile grows at my response. "Tell me about it," she murmurs, happily.

"Do you need any help?" I prompt. I love helping Hope, but sometimes she likes to do things alone. I always want to offer, yet, I don't want to force my assistance on her when sometimes she would rather do something herself. Although for something like this, there's a lot of ground to cover. We usually focus most of the outdoor decorations on the area where we place the Christmas tree for the tree lighting. We can't put anything inside the horse stables either because it's way too dangerous for the horses. Most of them will try to eat almost anything we put near them. But Hope likes to put lights and garland, accented with berries, bows or even pinecones on the outside of the fences as well as the stable, along with large wreaths on the sides of the barn and above the barn doors, as well as above the large iron blue star mounted above one of the small stables. She always finds a way to do something a little bit different though and at the same time, she keeps the same traditions she's had since she was a little girl.

She nods her head in acceptance, making me grateful. "Yeah, sure," she agrees. "I'm getting up at six to tack the horses, then I'll start decorating the area around here to get it ready for Sunday," she apprises me.

I sigh, hating that she's pushing herself so hard. She may not realize it, but I know exactly what she's doing. "Do you need me that early?" I question. There's no way I'll make it through the day if I start that early.

She shakes her head and waves me off, letting me know it's no big deal. "Nah. Whenever you want to come is fine," she replies.

"Great," I mumble, appreciatively. I take another bite of my sandwich, pondering what else I could do to show her I'm here for her. If she would let me, I'm confident I could really help her.

"Are your parents coming to the tree lighting?" she inquires.

I grin and remind her, "You know as well as I do they wouldn't miss it. Besides, they haven't been over to see your dad in a while," I add.

"I believe the Christmas tree is scheduled to be dropped off tomorrow," Hope announces, the excitement in her voice contagious.

"That's great," I murmur, softly.

"We'll have this place looking like Christmas in no time," she declares, proudly. She smiles wide, probably imagining what she wants it all to look like. I stare at her, my heart clenching at the beauty in her happiness.

Chapter 6

Gabe

I step through the front door of the inn and turn right making my way into the front office. I find Mr. McGregor in his usual spot behind the desk working on some paperwork. He looks up with a smile as I enter and nods his head towards me in greeting.

"I'm heading home for the night, Mr. McGregor," I inform him.

He furrows his eyebrows and questions, "You're not staying for dinner?"

I pinch my lips tightly together and shake my head in response, although I'd love to stay and eat with Hope. "Nah," I murmur. "I promised my mom I would help her put up the Christmas tree," I apprise him. I spend so much time here. I always make sure to set aside some time in my schedule for my family too, even if it's just helping out with something like putting up the Christmas tree. Family is extremely important to me.

"Ah," he utters, as he nods in understanding. He stands from the desk he's working at and saunters towards the front desk, stopping right in front of me. He places his palms on the front desk and casually murmurs, "Speaking of Christmas trees." He trails off and looks expectantly at me from across the desk, the corners of his mouth tugging upwards.

I chuckle softy and notify him, "I already told Hope that I would be here tomorrow to help, bright and early."

He nods his head in acknowledgement and gives me a big smile in approval. "Thanks, Gabe," he responds, appreciatively.

"No problem, Mr. McGregor," I reply. I'll be here to help as long as Hope lets me. He doesn't need to ask.

He smirks, obviously amused, but I'm not sure why. "Gabe you've known me for how long?" he questions.

My eyebrows draw down in confusion and I prompt, "Sir?"

"How long have you known me?" he repeats.

I shrug my shoulders and answer honestly, "I'd say my entire life."

He grins and nods his head in affirmation. "You're darn right. I drove your mom to the hospital when she was in labor with you and your Dad was stuck at work," he reiterates. It's the same story I've heard many times throughout my life.

"Yes, Sir, I remember the story," I acknowledge.

"You're what," he pauses briefly, thinking, "twenty-eight now?" he prompts.

I nod in confirmation. "Yes, that's right," I stammer.

He leans towards me and nods his head in verification. "I've known you twenty-eight years, Son," he emphasizes, "but you still call me Mr. McGregor," he accentuates.

I break out in a wide grin and breathe a sigh of relief, now that I understand the direction this conversation is going. "Old habits die hard," I proclaim.

"Call me Frank," he restates. "You make me feel like an old man when you call me Mr. McGregor," he claims.

My smile broadens. "Yes, Sir," I agree.

He groans and the corners of his mouth twitch up in amusement. "That's even worse!" he exclaims, teasing me.

I chuckle softly, amused by his reaction. "I don't know if I'll ever get used to calling you Frank," I admit, honestly.

"We'll work on it," he states. I nod in acknowledgement. "Have a good night, Gabe," he proclaims. Then he stands tall and makes his way back to his desk.

"You, too, Mr.," I pause and awkwardly correct myself, "Frank."

He chuckles and gives his head a light shake as I walk out the front door and down the steps. I stride around to the side of the inn and climb into my truck. I back out of the drive and pull onto the road, driving less than ten minutes before I'm home.

I pull into the gravel driveway behind my mom's black, crossover station wagon. I hop out of my truck and make my way to the front door of our pale grey farmhouse with black shutters and a small, open front porch. I climb up the five steps and walk through the front door, into our comfortable living room. We have a chocolate brown couch with colorful throw pillows scattered around it and two tan colored recliners, one on each end of the couch, all facing the flat screen TV sitting on top of the short, walnut entertainment center. The matching end tables each have a simple brass lamp, topped with an ivory lampshade, while the walnut coffee table remains empty, except for my dad's crossword puzzle book and one of my mom's cooking magazines. She's always looking for a new recipe to try out; either for here or for the restaurant she manages in our neighboring town.

"Mom, Dad, I'm home," I call out.

My mom walks out from the kitchen, her dark brown hair pulled up in a messy bun to keep it out of her face while cooking. She smiles at me as she wipes her hands on a red and white-checkered dishtowel. "Hi Gabriel," she murmurs, sounding tired.

I close the distance between us and lovingly place a kiss on the top of her head. "Hi, Mom. How was your day off?" I prompt.

"Good," she replies. "Dad took the day off with me, so we went out and got a few errands done," she informs me.

"Really?" I question, a little surprised. She nods in confirmation. The only times he usually takes off this time of year is to spend time with us or go Christmas shopping. He's always busy with making sure all end of the year numbers line up, as well as wrapping up all loose ends on different projects. "Did you do the kinds of errands that involve buying presents?" I tease, the corners of my mouth twitching up.

She giggles and shakes her head in amusement, but she doesn't answer my question. "Why don't you go wash up for dinner?" she suggests. "Your dad and I are just finishing everything up," she informs me.

"Okay," I agree. "I'll be right there," I add. I make my way down the hallway and slip into my bedroom. I drop the keys to my truck on my tall, pine dresser to my right as I walk into the room and pull out a simple black t-shirt to change into, not wanting to wear a dirty shirt to the dinner table. I toss my dirty clothes into my hamper, in the corner of my closet. Then I turn to walk out of my room, noticing my gray comforter accented with pale yellow is pulled up neatly over my sheets, even though I never made my bed. I try, but most mornings I leave so early to help feed the animals, I rush out before I have a chance to get it done. "Thanks, Mom," I mumble to myself. I walk across the hall to the bathroom, and try to scrub all the dirt and grime off my hands from a full day at the ranch.

I make my way back down the hall and into our cranberry red, white and navy blue, country style kitchen, where I find both of my parents sitting at our small, pine kitchen table, waiting for me. "Hi, Dad," I greet him. I have my mom's brown, wavy hair, but I look so much like my dad. We have the same emerald green eyes and the same build with broad shoulders and a narrow waist, although he's two inches taller than me at six feet. We even have the same dimpled chin. My dad's dark blonde hair is now speckled with a touch of grey. He's dressed down today in dark blue jeans and a simple dark green long sleeved shirt.

"Hi, Son. How's everything at the ranch?" he probes.

"Good," I mumble, as I lower myself into the seat between them. I inhale deeply, enjoying the scent of the roasted chicken, baked potatoes and grilled asparagus. "This looks delicious," I mumble to both of them. "Thank you," I add, sincerely.

"Have you started decorating the ranch for the holidays?" Mom inquires, the excitement clear in her voice. My mom and Frank have been best friends for a long time. She used to go to the ranch every Christmas as a child and wanted to continue the tradition with her family. When we were kids I'd go to the ranch after school and play with Hope and Joy, while my parents were at work. Then after work, many times my parents would come to pick me up and we'd all end up staying and having dinner with the McGregor's, like they were our second family. Then as we got older, I started helping out on the ranch, alongside both of them.

When Hope and Joy's mom died, both my mom and dad increased their visits to the ranch, doing everything they could for Frank, as well as the girls. They don't make it there as often as they used to, but with me there every day, they always know if the McGregor's need anything and do whatever they can to help. I know she misses it sometimes, but I think at Christmastime, she looks forward to going to see all the Christmas decorations at the ranch more than anything else. She used to tell me, just being there this time of year can be a little nostalgic for her.

"They've done a little bit inside the inn and the front porch, but we're starting on the outside tomorrow morning," I reveal. "I promised Hope I'd be there early to help," I add. Although, I'm sure both of them assumed that's exactly where I would be. Everyone knows how I feel about Hope. Well, everyone except maybe Hope and I can't seem to figure out a way to tell her.

"Your mom and I picked out a Christmas tree last night," my dad informs me, redirecting the conversation.

I give him a small, grateful smile and nod my head in acknowledgement. "Yeah, mom told me. That's why she wanted me to come home early tonight," I enlighten him, with a small shrug. "To help decorate and set up the tree," I add.

He nods in understanding. "So, after dinner, will you help me bring it in from out back?" he requests.

"Absolutely," I concur, with a firm nod. He smiles in acknowledgement and then he takes a bite of his chicken.

"So," my mom begins, hesitantly. I quirk my eyebrow at her and wait to see what she wants to say. It's rare you find her edging into a conversation like she is now. "Do you think you might be picking out a tree with Hope one of these years?" she probes, not being the least bit discreet. I feel the heat rush to my face, instantly turning my cheeks red. She gives me a sad smile and continues. "It's just, we want you to be happy, Gabriel," she stammers.

I heave a sigh and mumble, "I know, Mom, but you know what Hope has been through," I remind her. She nods sadly in confirmation. I take a deep breath and answer her as honestly as I can without having a conversation with Hope because the truth is, I don't know what she thinks about me, about us anymore. "I always thought Hope and I would be married and have our own house by now," I admit. "I thought we'd be picking out and decorating our own Christmas tree together. Of course I'll be helping her decorate at the ranch and helping you guys here, but I know what you're getting at, Mom and you're right," I acknowledge. I pause, thinking about where I was with Hope before the accident and how it feels like we're at a complete standstill now. I look at Hope like she's my whole world, but I'm not even sure how she feels about me. "But that's just not our reality. We're not married. We're not engaged. Heck, we're not even dating," I concede, regretfully. My chest aches, painfully, as I vocalize obvious facts about the relationship between the two of us.

"Gabe," my mom begins, sympathetically.

I shake my head, stopping her from continuing. I drop my fork down on my plate, letting it clatter. I don't want to listen to this right now. I can't. I wish things were different between us. I'm trying to help her and hoping she wants me in her life as much as I want her in mine. I want to be the one to help her move on from it all, but she needs to be ready to do that. I can't force her or drag her through it. "It's fine, Mom," I grumble. "I just need a minute," I claim. I push my chair back, scraping it, loudly, against the wood floor. I plant my hands on my knees and push, standing up from the table and immediately stride for the back door. I throw it open and step out into the back yard, shutting the door much more forcefully than necessary.

I take a deep breath and drop my head back, tilting it up towards the sky. The stars shine brightly in the blackened night sky and I focus on the first one I see. I close my eyes and make a wish on the star, just like I used to do with Hope and Joy when we were kids. "My only wish, Hope, is for you to be happy again," I whisper into the silence. "That's all I ever want." My heart clenches tightly, aching to make her dreams come true. I still believe I'm the one that can help make it happen. For my sake, I have to.

A light breeze whistles in the air, spreading goosebumps over my arms. I open my eyes, acknowledging the cold with a heavy sigh. I love Hope and I want to share everything with her. At this point, either she feels the same way I do, or maybe I need to find a way to move on. I gulp down the growing lump in my throat at just the thought of letting her go. I honestly don't know if I could ever do it if I had to. My stomach growls, reminding me I walked out during dinner. I take one more deep breath before I turn back towards the house and pull the back door open. I step back inside the kitchen, welcoming the warmth, as I close the door behind me. I'll figure it out soon enough. I have to.

Chapter 7

Hope

I double-check the knot in my red, white and green striped apron before I pick up the red and white platter full of Christmas cookies. I inhale deeply enjoying the prevalent scent of sugar and spice as I push through the kitchen door and into the dining area. I pass by a ten-year-old boy, with black hair and big brown eyes, who's here with his parents and two older sisters. He's holding a small, round, white plate piled high with two brownies, a red frosted Christmas cookie and a slice of apple pie. I smile at him while I make my way to the wall of cabinets we use for self-serving and place the platter in an empty spot on the counter. The boy slips in behind me, just as the plate touches the white, granite countertop. He grabs another cookie from the edge of the platter, making me laugh. He grins wide, showcasing his gap-toothed smile. "You have the best cookies!" he announces, emphatically.

"Thank you," I reply, returning his smile.

He spins around and strolls back to the table, joining the rest of his family. I turn back to the counter and assess the rest of the area. A stack of clean, white plates still remains on one end, with the coffee and tea carafes on the other, still half full and the dessert platters and pie dishes spread out in between. Above the counter we have a long, single, raised shelf, organized with napkins, silverware, decorations, and clean mugs, in plain white as well as various red and green, decorative, holiday mugs. The decorations include a porcelain red and white stocking, an oval gingerbread man platter, and colorful holiday signs for hot cocoa as well as one for cookies and milk. Garland made with small red, green and silver ornaments loops underneath the shelf, bringing everything together.

I turn to my right, towards the tall, tiered bistro table, leaning up against the wall. It's classically accessorized with red and green velvet bows on each tier. The middle shelf has decorative bowls still full of fresh fruit and smaller ones filled with holiday candies on the bottom. I continue around the room, admiring the decorations and checking on the guests as I go. The guests are seated around the room at round dining tables, all covered with a Christmas green tablecloth and a white pillar candle surrounded by a holly ring as the centerpiece at each. Three to five white, wooden chairs with high backs accented with a beautiful red and green plaid bow are placed at each one and all the tables are filled with guests. Mounted on the walls on each side of the room, we wrapped the framed pictures with colorful, festive wrapping paper and added a bow in the center, to make the art look like Christmas presents. Around the sliding glass door leading out onto the patio decorated with white twinkle lights, we have country style garland, with several handmade, miniature snowmen hanging along the length of it.

"Hope," Mrs. Elkhart calls my name, bringing my attention to her. I step closer to her table and smile warmly at her. "Thank you so much for accommodating me and Lee for dinner," she tells me, appreciatively. "I'm so glad we were able to stay a little longer," she proclaims with a wide grin. She nods in her husband's direction, before looking back at me.

"No problem, Mrs. Elkhart," I reply, returning her smile. "You've been coming up here for as long as I can remember. We'd never say no to you," I insist.

"You're so sweet," she whispers. "Well, I have to tell you," she begins, "that pumpkin pie was absolutely divine," she compliments, with a lick of her lips. "It was just like your mother used to make it," she praises.

I gasp at the mention of my mom. I feel my body instantly go rigid with anxiety. I know I probably should have expected someone to mention my mom; someone always does, especially because I use mom's recipes all the time for special occasions. I force myself to smile, loving her compliment, but also aching with the reminder. I can't help but wonder if it will ever stop feeling this way, bittersweet. "It's her recipe," I enlighten her. "I'm glad I was able to remind you of her," I claim. My stomach begins tying itself in knots, even though my statement is true. I want everyone to remember her for how amazing she was, but that doesn't make it hurt any less when there's a reminder of her.

"Where is your sister?" she questions. She looks around the room and peaks around the corner, as if she might jump out from somewhere. "I wanted to say goodbye," she adds, bringing her gaze back to me.

My shoulders slowly relax with the change of subject. "She went to the train station to pick up a new guest," I reveal.

"Oh," she grumbles. She grimaces, obviously disappointed. "Well, you will give her a hug for me, won't you?" she requests.

I nod in agreement and respond, "Of course."

Mrs. Elkhart pushes her chair back, sliding it on the wood floor and then stands up. Her husband, Lee, follows her lead, instantly rising out of his seat. She takes a step towards me and wraps me in a tight hug. I immediately lift my arms and return her hug, before I gently release her. She smiles and proclaims, "It's always good seeing you, Hope."

"You too," I insist. "Same time next year?" I prompt.

She nods in confirmation. "We wouldn't miss it. Right, Lee?" she prompts, twisting her body around to give her attention to her husband.

Mr. Elkart is about the same height as my dad, but he has a leaner build with thick, gray hair, pale blue eyes and a kind smile. He's dressed in faded blue jeans and a blue and white flannel shirt, buttoned up and tucked in, showcasing his gold buckle. He grins and nods his head firmly, immediately agreeing with his wife. "That's right," he reiterates, with a step in our direction.

"That's great!" I declare, murmuring my satisfaction. "Well, you folks have a safe drive home," I tell them.

"And you have a very Merry Christmas," Mrs. Elkhart states, cheerfully.

"Merry Christmas to you, too!" I add.

I wave to both of them, before Lee takes a step towards the exit. I immediately begin clearing the table as Mrs. Elkhart turns to follow her husband, but then stops to talk to another one of our repeat guests, as Lee patiently waits for her. I spin on my heel and stride towards the kitchen with their dirty dishes in my hands.

I step into the kitchen and place the dishes in the sink, right next to where dad is already at work cleaning the pots. "I got this, Dad," I offer.

He chuckles softly as he continues to wash the stainless steel stockpot in his hands. "Take the night off, Hope," he encourages, barely glancing in my direction.

I ignore his comment and maintain, "Really, I got it. You should go say goodbye to the Elkharts," I suggest.

He sets the clean pot in his hands down and glances at me, drying his hands on a red hand towel. "They're all done already?" he questions.

I nod in confirmation. "Yup," I proclaim, popping the p. "Mr. Elkhart got up from the table," I enlighten him.

He chuckles softly and gives a small shake of his head. "Yeah, that's his signal that they're ready to go," he concedes.

"Go see them off, Dad," I repeat.

"You sure?" he prompts.

I nod in confirmation and offer him a small smile to let him know it's okay. "Yeah, I got this," I reiterate.

He grins back at me, as he sets down the clean pot on a red and green-checkered dishtowel. "Thanks, Honey," he acknowledges, appreciatively. He leans down and kisses me lovingly on the top of my head, causing me to smile to myself.

I pick up a large platter and begin working my way through the pile of dirty dishes sitting in front of me, as he walks out of the kitchen. I can't help, but think about what Mrs. Elkhart said about the pie. Those thoughts soon let my mind wander to thoughts of my mom as I clean. I remember the first time Joy and I were in the kitchen helping her make the same pumpkin pie I made today. I was so excited when she gave us both aprons. Then, she gave me my own bowl and pie dish, while she had Joy helping with her bowl. I was so careful to copy her every move, but Joy just kept asking if it was time for her to taste it yet. I chuckle softly at the memory. Some things never change.

I exhale slowly, my heart aching. I miss her so much. It still hurts so much when someone even mentions her, but that's also the way I want it to be. I want people to be able to talk about her, and share stories about her and of course stories about my Aunt Faith too.

I want to keep their memories alive. I guess that's why I make my mom's pumpkin pie every year. It's a small way for me to feel close to her and to keep her memory alive in my eyes and hopefully in the eyes of everyone around me. Now I just need the strength to talk about it.

I reach for a pale blue dishtowel embroidered with white snowflakes. Then I grab one of the plates I just finished washing and run the towel around it, drying it. I put the dishes away and continue cleaning up the rest of the kitchen, as my thoughts turn to Gabe. He's never really pushed me before about leaving the ranch, not like he did today. He's always let me do everything at my own pace, but today everything felt different. Was it because he asked me out to dinner? Was he asking me on a date or just to go as friends? I shake my head and tell myself he was probably just trying to help me like he always does.

My heart skips a beat as I think about how much Gabe really does for me. It's incredible how he's always there for me. Maybe I could handle leaving the ranch with him? I know he would be there for me every step of the way and I don't want to keep disappointing him like I did today. The look on his face when I didn't respond to his offer broke my heart. I do think about getting in his truck with him and pulling out of the driveway to go somewhere, anywhere, but the thought alone causes me to sway on my feet and my stomach to churn. I heave a heavy sigh and admit to myself, I don't think I can do it. I don't think I'm ready. I have to figure out a way to push myself though. If I keep waiting, Gabe might not always be there to protect me. Chills spread down my spine as a wave of nausea washes over me at the thought of my life without Gabe. I cringe at the mere idea. That's not something I ever want to imagine. I can't let that become my reality.

I move around the kitchen, putting all the clean dishes back in the cabinets. I finish with the last pile of plates, just as my dad walks back in with another stack of dirty dishes. "Everyone is gone," he announces. He sets the pile down next to the sink and suggests, "How about you finish up in here and I'll start clearing the dining room?"

"That sounds good, Dad," I reply. "Thanks," I add, giving him a grateful smile. He grins and nods his head in acknowledgment, before he turns to walk back out into the other room. "Dad," I call out, stopping him in his tracks.

He slowly turns back around, to face me, with his eyebrows arched in question. "Yes?" he prompts.

I look at him and fight the tears wanting to overflow. I gulp down the growing lump in my throat and take a deep breath. "I love you," I whisper. With my thoughts consumed by mom and Gabe, I feel a strong urge to vocalize how I feel to him.

He pauses, giving me a look of pure love and adoration. "I love you too, Hope," he rasps. He swiftly closes the distance between us and wraps me up in his arms, hugging me tightly. I lean into his embrace, wrapping my arms around his waist, feeling overwhelmed with his love and protection. Then he leans back, and lovingly places a kiss on the top of my head, before he releases me. I let my hands slide away from him, as I watch him turn around and walk back into the dining area to finish clearing the tables.

I take a deep breath and exhale slowly, trying to pull myself back together. I admit to myself, the only other time I feel so incredibly safe and loved is when I'm with Gabe. I don't ever want to lose him, but I have no idea what that means for us, or even for me.

I feel a nudge at my leg and look down. Kody, our yellow lab and Oliver our black lab and doxy mix, both sit tall, wagging their tails at me, requesting my attention. Although, Oliver sitting up is still pretty small. He's short and even a little stubby, but absolutely adorable. I giggle in spite of everything, seeing their happy, furry faces. "Are you two looking for scraps?" I prompt. I crouch down and scratch them both behind the ears. I stand and grab a treat out of the white ceramic dog treats jar. I offer one to each of them, feeling a sense of calm as they both carefully snatch up the treat. It amazes me what a little bit of love from an animal can do for a person.

Chapter 8

Joy

I pull up to the remote train station between Evergreen Valley and the next town over and drive right up to the front. I park along the curb, noticing one car behind me and one car in front of me doing the same thing. I hop out and lean against my navy blue SUV, crossing my feet at my ankles. I look up at the three-story train station, with glass windows most of the way up. Large block lettering, stating, "Transportation Center" is written down the front of the building to the right, from the top floor all the way down. I stuff my hands in my pockets to keep them warm as I hear the whistle of the train and the screech of the brakes as it pulls in. I quickly glance at my phone, checking the time, before I slide it back in my pocket. Then I watch the front doors leading to and from the platform, looking for a man from the city. I wonder if I'll be able to figure out which one he is. Then again, there are never a lot of people getting off the train by Evergreen Valley and I usually know the ones who do.

A handful of passengers begin exiting the building and walking in different directions to make their way to their cars or meeting someone picking them up. Suddenly, a tall, fit, good-looking man with dark brown hair and bronzed skin strides outside, nearly stumbling out the door with all his luggage. He's dressed in black, designer skinny jeans and a blue button-down dress shirt, looking a little lost and completely out of place. My heart skips a beat at the sight of him, but it's not like I haven't met a good-looking man before. I smirk and roll my eyes at how out of place he looks and chuckle to myself in response. Of course I know which one he is. I push off my car and quickly close the distance between us. "Ethan Dulane?" I question.

His hazel eyes, surrounded by dark, long lashes widen in surprise. He looks around as if he's looking for someone before he looks back at me, helping me notice a touch of gold in his eyes. "Yes, that's me," he finally confirms, as if he's unsure.

I fight to hold back my laughter and arch my eyebrows in challenge. Then I prod, "You don't know your own name?"

"Excuse me?" he prods, perplexed.

"You looked around like it was someone else. Are you sure you're Ethan Dulane?" I question, a teasing tone to my voice.

He chuckles nervously and gives a shake of his head. "Yes, I'm Ethan Dulane," he affirms. "And you are?" he inquires.

"Joy McGregor," I inform him, confidently. "Welcome to Evergreen Valley." I hold my hand out to him and smile.

He fumbles with his bags to free his right hand. He clasps my hand and gives it a shake, sending what feels like a shock of electricity up my arm, but I attempt to ignore it. "Thank you," he mumbles, as he grins back at me.

"Are you ready?" I inquire.

"Yes," he concurs. "Is there a limo or something?" he questions, as he looks past my SUV and into the nearly empty parking lot just beyond.

I can't stop my laughter from spilling out, but I quickly catch my breath. "Limo?" I prod, my eyes wide with disbelief. I shake my head, my response playful, "No, you're not in the city anymore, Mr. Dulane."

"Ethan, please," he requests.

"I'm your ride," I enlighten him.

"You?" he probes.

I smirk and confirm, "Yes. Is that a problem?" I challenge.

"No, no of course not," he blurts out, shaking his head in denial. "But where's the car?" he prompts.

I grin, amused by his reaction. I glance behind me at my SUV before looking back at him with a question in my eyes. "You're looking at it," I announce.

I grab both of his suitcases, with a small bag strapped on top of the larger one and roll them over to the tailgate of my SUV. He hesitates, surprised with my answer. "Oh," he murmurs.

I open the back and set the small bag inside, before I hoist the large suitcase into the back. "Something wrong?" I prod, arching my eyebrows in challenge.

He shakes his head, "No! Let me get that for you," he offers, finally moving and taking a step towards me.

"I already got it," I declare.

Ethan takes another step towards me as I lift his other suitcase into the truck. He nods in acknowledgement. Then he asks, "Mind if I keep my suit in the back seat?"

My eyes widen in surprise. With my disbelief clear, I question, "You brought a suit?" I giggle, not even trying to hide my amusement.

"Yeah, in case there's a fancy function or something," he mumbles, attempting to defend himself.

I slam the tailgate closed and then look at him. "Well, I hate to break it to you, Mr. Dulane, but you're

68

staying on a working ranch. We only wear suits to weddings and funerals up here. So, unless you're considering getting married," I trail off, smirking.

His eyes widen in surprise and something else. He shakes his head in denial and quickly blurts out, "No! No, definitely not. Or dying. Hah," he falters.

I grin, looking him up and down and shake my head in amusement. "Well, hop on in," I encourage him. "Go ahead and put your suit in the back seat," I instruct.

"Thanks," he mumbles. He opens the door and hangs his suit in the back on a small hook near the door, as I climb in behind the wheel. He steps back and looks around, making sure he has everything.

"You coming?" I prompt.

"Oh, right. Yeah. Sorry," he stammers.

He closes the back door. Then he glances at the side of the car and tilts his head to the side, probably noticing our name and logo on the side, "Two Sisters Ranch". He pulls the front door open and slides into the passenger seat, slamming the door behind him.

I buckle my seat belt and wait for him to do the same. I pull away from the curb and out of the parking lot before I allow my curiosity to get the best of me. "So, what brings you to Two Sisters Ranch?" I probe, curiously.

He sighs heavily, as he settles into the passenger seat. "My publisher thought it would be good for me," he claims.

"Publisher? You a writer or something?" I prod.

"Or something," he mutters. He heaves another sigh and then admits, "I've had a bit of a struggle coming up with my next story."

"Oh," I murmur, dragging out the word. "Writer's block," I state in understanding.

"It's not Writer's Block," he declares, sounding defensive. "I'm just having a hard time with ideas," he claims.

I don't bother fighting my amusement as I watch the dark road stretched out in front of me. I confidently reaffirm, "Sounds like Writer's Block to me."

He grimaces and then shakes his head. "Anyway," he begins, ignoring my comment, "my publisher thought I could get some inspiration up here," he enlightens me.

I can't stop my giggle from escaping. His casual statement reminds me of the horses. "I can show you Inspiration in the morning if you'd like," I tease, even though he's not in on my joke.

"Really? You think you have inspiration for me?" he prompts, seriously.

"Oh, I know I do," I announce, confidently.

"You don't even know what I write," he mutters, his confusion obvious.

"Okay, then. What do you write?" I ask, humoring him.

"I specialize in adventure romance novels," he informs me.

"Really?" I prod. I glance in his direction before immediately bringing my focus back to the road. "That's interesting," I murmur. "I bet my sister has read them," I proclaim. "She loves those kinds of books," I emphasize.

He arches his eyebrows in challenge. "Those kinds of books?" he questions, arching his eyebrow. "What's that supposed to mean?" he challenges.

I grimace and shake my head, attempting to dismiss my own comment. "Oh, nothing. It's just really not my type of story," I explain, with a shrug of my shoulders.

"What is?" he asks.

"I'm more of a horror kind of girl," I admit.

"Interesting choice. I wouldn't have pegged you for a horror fan," he mumbles, a small smile on his face.

"Don't get me wrong, I hate horror movies," I add, defensively.

"Really?" he probes, surprised. Then he mumbles something under his breath I can't quite make out.

I arch my eyebrow in question, but he doesn't say anything else, so I answer his question. "Yeah. I can't stand the sight of gore," I concede, scrunching my nose up in disgust at the thought. "It's much scarier in my imagination," I claim.

He laughs, the sound vibrating over me and jump-starting my heart. "Okay, I can appreciate that," he concedes. "So, you have a sister?" he prompts.

"Yes. Her name is Hope," I answer.

He grins and chuckles softly. "Joy and Hope. That's cute," he claims.

"My parents planned it that way. My mom's name was Grace," I add. A thoughtful smile touches my face as her name passes through my lips.

"Was?" he prods, a touch of concern in his voice.

"Yeah," I confirm, nodding my head. "She died five years ago in a car wreck," I reveal, continuing to stare straight ahead.

"I'm so sorry," he states, apologetically.

"Thanks," I reply, reflexively and force a smile. My thoughts briefly drift to my mom, while Ethan sits quietly next to me.

He finally breaks the silence. "So, Two Sisters Ranch. I take it the ranch is named after you and your sister?" he questions.

"No, actually," I correct, a smile playing upon my lips. We hear the same assumption quite often. "My grandparents started the ranch back in the sixties and named it for my mom and aunt; Two Sisters."

"Wow. That's really cool," he proclaims. "Does your aunt work there, too?" he asks.

I wince slightly and take a deep breath. "No, she was killed with my mom," I explain, matter of fact.

I notice him close his eyes in regret with my words. He sighs in defeat. His cheeks slightly pink in embarrassment for accidentally sticking his foot in his mouth again. "I'm sorry," he mumbles, with clear empathy in his voice. "I'm just ruining this conversation," he grumbles.

"No, it's fine," I claim, shaking my head. "You didn't know. People ask about it all the time," I concede.

"I'm sure they do," he murmurs and nods in understanding.

"My grandparents retired to Florida once the wreck happened. They couldn't stand being in town anymore," I add, honestly.

"I can understand that," he mumbles.

"So it's me, Hope and my dad. We've got a few stable hands and people helping out, but the only consistent one is Gabe," I inform him.

"Gabe?" he questions.

"Yeah," I confirm. "You'll meet him, I'm sure. His mom is my dad's best friend. We all grew up together. He's like a brother to me," I explain, revealing more than even I expected.

"Oh. Nice. Small town vibes," he murmurs.

"You can say that," I reply.

He nods in acknowledgement. Then he turns and looks out the window into the endless dark of night, while I continue to drive towards the ranch. He seems like a nice guy and he's definitely handsome. It could be a lot of fun while he's here.

Chapter 9

Ethan

I see a break in the darkness and bring my gaze in that direction, just as Joy turns towards the light. A large farmhouse comes into view, with its white Christmas lights and thick green garland, strung along the front porch across the top and along each pole. Lights from all around the house shine through the windows, lighting it up even more. The whole image in front of me reminds me of something I would find on the front of a Christmas card.

As Joy pulls around a circular driveway, I notice another light off to my right and glance in that direction, seeing a small cape-like house with a high roofline. There's no front porch, but it has massive French doors for the front door, with large picture windows on each side and white lights outlining the whole house, reminding me of a gingerbread house. "That's the carriage house," she informs me.

I nod my head in acknowledgement, as she stops in front of the expansive home I first saw, surrounded mostly by open space and trees, from what I can tell. I look around, trying to take in my surroundings and soon realize this must be the Inn part of the ranch in front of me. It's absolutely beautiful, but it really feels like it's in the middle of nowhere. It's hard to see too much beyond the inn and the carriage house. I guess I'm just not used to so much country.

Joy shifts her car into park and shuts it off. "Here we are," she announces. She looks past me towards the inn, with a sparkle in her eyes.

"Wow. Rustic," I murmur, attempting to take it all in. I can't believe how pitch black everything really is out here.

"Trust me, you'll love it," she claims, her pride clear in the sweet sound of her voice.

"It's a far cry from Manhattan, that's for sure," I comment, stating the obvious.

She giggles, the sound sending chills down my spine. Then she looks at me and offers, "Come on, I'll get you settled."

She unbuckles her seatbelt and jumps out of the truck. I do the same and follow with my briefcase slung over my shoulder. We both walk around to the back of the truck and she opens the tailgate. "I got it," I declare. I don't need her to take my bags for me again. She's going to think I can't do anything for myself. I reach into the truck to grab my suitcase at the same time she does. My hand brushes hers, shooting tingles up my arm.

"I can do it," she proclaims. "I'm used to this," she insists. Her confidence practically radiates off of her and it's stunning.

"But it's my stuff," I remind her, defiantly. I shouldn't let her grab my suitcases for me again. I'm not helpless.

"You're my guest," she emphasizes, arguing.

"I insist," I reiterate.

She clenches her teeth and narrows her eyes, staring at me as if she wants to say more. "Fine," she grumbles, finally relenting. She takes a step back.

I clasp my suitcase and yank it out of her car, giving myself more momentum than I mean to. Suddenly, I lose my balance and I feel myself falling. I barely flail my arms, trying to catch myself, already knowing it's no use. I gasp and tumble to the ground, landing hard on my backside, with my suitcase falling next to me with a thud. My eyes widen in shock and I feel my face heat instantly in embarrassment. I glance at Joy, hoping she missed my fall, at the same time, already knowing she not only saw everything, she had the best seat in the house.

Her eyes widen with surprise. I notice her bite her lip, in an obvious attempt to hold back her laughter. "Oh, my gosh!" she exclaims. "Are you okay?" she prompts.

"Yeah," I mutter, fighting back a groan. I can only imagine what kind of impression I'm making on this woman. She's absolutely beautiful and obviously a strong, independent woman, which makes her even more attractive, while I'm making a complete fool of myself.

"Here, let me help you," she offers. She reaches her hand down towards me offering her assistance. I swallow my pride and gratefully accept it, enveloping her small hand in mine. Her surprisingly strong grip helps me pull myself off the cold hard ground.

I stand in front of her and grin down at her, having about six inches on her. She returns my smile. The extreme beauty of her big, bright, blue eyes suddenly overwhelms me. "Thanks," I mumble, still holding her hand.

She stares back at me for a moment, before she finally pulls her hand back. I immediately feel the loss of her warmth. "Why don't you get your suit, Mr. Dulane?" she suggests. "I'll take care of your bags."

I take a deep breath, enjoying the fresh country air. I exhale slowly and give myself a mental shake, pulling myself out of my daze. "My suit. Right," I stammer. "I

75

almost forgot." I grab the bathroom bag and slip it over my shoulder. Then I pick up my briefcase with my laptop and all my paperwork inside and sling it over the same shoulder. I hurry around the truck and grab my suit out of the back seat and close the door, while Joy grabs my suitcases. She pulls them up the driveway and I follow right behind her.

We step onto the front porch and I can't help, but smile at the rocking chairs to my right. Rocking chairs on a front porch make me think of a country home and lasting love, like a couple ending each day together, talking about their day, side by side in their rocking chairs overlooking their land. I love that they have them here. We step inside and walk through a small foyer and turn to the right, walking into a front office. A big man, about my parents' age, stands behind the front desk, leaning on his hands, looking down at something in front of him.

"Hi, Daddy," Joy says, in greeting.

He lifts his gaze to hers and grins broadly, causing me to immediately see the resemblance. "Hi there, Joy," he proclaims. He ambles around the desk, with a slight limp and greets her with a hug. He releases her and straightens, making me realize how big he really is. He turns his attention towards me. "And you must be Ethan," he states, politely. He reaches his hand out and I grasp it, shaking his hand. "I'm Frank McGregor," he informs me, introducing himself.

"Nice to meet you," I declare before I release his hand.

"Likewise. Welcome to Two Sisters Ranch," he adds, with a proud grin.

"Thank you for having me," I reply.

"Have you had dinner yet?" he questions.

I try to ignore my grumbling stomach at the mention of food and give him a crooked smile. I hesitantly admit, "If you count the bag of chips on the train, then yes."

He chuckles and shakes his head. Then he looks towards his daughter and begins, "Joy, why don't you..."

"Already on it," she interrupts. "Where's Hope?" she prompts.

"I think she's in the kitchen," he enlightens her.

"Okay," she acknowledges. She turns to leave and I stop myself from reaching out to hold her back.

"Where are you going?" I inquire.

"To fix you some dinner," she responds, as if I should already know the answer.

My eyebrows draw down in confusion. "But," I begin, uncertainly, "I haven't ordered anything," I remind her.

She throws her head back and bursts out laughing, the sound causing my heart to skip a beat. "This is a ranch, Mr. Dulane. You eat what you're served," she states, leaving no room for argument. She winks at me, the corners of her mouth twitching up in amusement. Then she spins on her heel and strides out of the room. I bite my lip, fighting an amused grin.

"Joy's my youngest," Frank informs me, nodding his head in the direction she went. "She's a spitfire," he proudly claims.

"I can tell," I reply.

"Amanda Parkington already took care of your room, so here is your key," he announces, as he hands me a room key, "and your activities list for the week," he explains. He hands me a flyer entitled, "Two Sisters Ranch Activities," with a list of the week's activities written in red and green and adorned with festive holiday clip art.

My eyebrows draw down in confusion as I scan the sheet in my hand, wondering if Amanda signed me up for something without telling me. I tilt my head to the side and look up at him. "Activities?" I prompt.

He nods in acknowledgement and elaborates. "Activities we offer here at the ranch, like hiking, hay rides and of course, riding the trails," he adds.

"What about lessons?" I inquire. I know I have to find a way to throw myself into ranch life to get a better understanding of what happens on a ranch, especially if I want to write a good book. I'm not about to let this trip be a waste of time for anyone now that I'm here.

"Never rode a horse, huh?" he probes, smiling politely. I shake my head in response, feeling my cheeks heat at my admission. "Yeah, I'm sure Hope or Joy can help you out," he offers.

I breathe a sigh of relief and mumble, "Good."

"We actually have a lot of Christmas activities this month too, plus our annual tree lighting on Friday night," he adds. "You don't have to do anything if you don't want to, but Ms. Parkington asked me to help you become one with the community," he announces, smirking at me. He shrugs and mumbles, "Whatever that means."

"For inspiration," I murmur my simple answer.

Frank laughs out loud. When he catches his breath, he jokes, "You'll get Inspiration in the morning, I'm sure."

My eyebrows draw further down, puzzled by his reaction. "That's what Joy said," I apprise him, surprised by the repeated comment.

"Well, she will take good care of you," he claims. He points towards the stairs in the foyer and instructs, "Your room is upstairs and down the hall to the left. Why don't you set down your belongings, then go to the dining room for dinner?" he suggests.

I sigh and nod in agreement, suddenly feeling both tired and hungry. "Sure. That sounds great. I'm starving," I concede.

"Well, Hope is a great cook," he praises. "That's my oldest," he adds as explanation.

"Joy told me," I inform him.

"Great," he declares. "The dining room is at the end of that hall," he directs, gesturing past the stairs and to the right.

"Thanks, Frank," I murmur, grateful for his hospitality. I may have ended up somewhere unexpected today, but at least I'll be comfortable.

"You're welcome," he replies.

I turn around and grab my suitcases and my bags. I awkwardly make my way towards the stairs and carefully begin climbing with my hands full, not wanting to make another trip. I trudge down the hallway, covered with a dark green runner and find my room at the very end of the hall on the left, as directed. I set my bags down and use the key to unlock the door. I push the door open and stand in front of it, while I pull my bags inside. I close the door and pull my bags all the way into the room, walking past a spacious full bathroom, before I step into a large bedroom with pale yellow, almost ivory colored walls. The moment I walk in, I set the key down to my left on a long, antique white dresser, with a decorative mirror mounted on top of it. Just beyond the dresser is a small closet. I walk over to it and hang up my leather coat. I step away from the closet and glance out the window right behind me, noticing another house that appears similar to this one, but smaller off the back. I wonder if it's part of the inn? I pull my focus back to the room, walking towards an old oak work desk. This will be perfect for writing. I walk over to my bags and grab my briefcase. I carry it across the room and set it down next to the desk. I reach in and pull my laptop out, immediately setting it on the desk. I look across the room at the king sized bed with a beautiful antique white headboard and footboard, with short, rounded posts at each corner. The room looks festive, accented with a Christmas wreath hanging over the bed and Christmas decorations on the matching nightstands on each side of the bed. I can't help but think this room is bigger than my apartment at home.

I glance over at my bags and grimace as my stomach growls. "Unpacking can wait," I mumble to myself. I walk past my suitcases and grab the room key off the dresser, slipping it into my pocket. Then I turn and immediately stride out the door, pulling it closed behind me. "I need to eat," I add.

Chapter 10

Joy

I lean my hip against the black and gray speckled, granite countertops in our newly renovated kitchen off the back of the Inn. I watch as Hope quickly throws some food together to make Ethan some dinner. Hope is an amazing cook and she deserves to have a kitchen she can really work in with everything she does for both guests and staff at the inn, the ranch and for our family for that matter. The kitchen is long with massive cream cabinets, enhanced with beautiful moldings and black iron handles on the bottom cabinets and knobs on the top. She rotates the chicken in the pan on the glass top stove, with a large hood overhead. Behind her is a large kitchen island with a deep, stainless, farm sink and the dishwasher right next to it. Stools are pushed in on the other side, with plenty of space for counter seating. To the right, when facing the back, is the massive, stainless steel refrigerator and on the wall opposite, a double oven. Between the two appliances is a small hallway leading to a walk-in pantry and then into a small dining room for our family and in extremely rare occasions for our guests. Off to the left of the island is a large, rectangular, oak dining table with a bench on the far side against a half wall, leading down into a small family room with a gray couch, love seat and entertainment center with a TV. Windows and a sliding glass door cover the back wall, leading out to one of our horse stables.

I grab a fork and begin picking at the mashed potatoes on the stove, while I watch Hope put a plate together for Ethan. "He's a real city slicker," I claim.

She glances up at me and gives me a look. Then she narrows her eyes and warns me, "You better be nice to him, Joy. He's staying for two weeks," she enlightens me.

My eyes widen and my heart skips a beat at the thought of him being here for so long. Maybe I'll be able to spend a lot of time with him. "Two weeks!" I exclaim. I grin and jokingly mutter, "Maybe I'll make a country boy out of him after all."

Hope gives me another look of warning. "Joy..." she mutters, trailing off.

"What?" I question, innocently and shrug my shoulders. "He's handsome," I admit, wiggling my eyebrows. She rolls her eyes in response. I continue, needing to say more. "And he's different than all the guys that are around here," I contend.

She stops and narrows her eyes at me. "There's nothing wrong with the guys around here," she asserts, defensively.

I wave her off and instantly proclaim, "I didn't mean Gabe." I know exactly what she's thinking. I walk around the counter and sit down on one of the stools on the end of the island. I put my forearms on the counter and lean on them. "He's different," I insist.

"Joy, stop," she protests. She shakes her head, as her cheeks turn slightly pink. She turns towards the stove, giving me her back, obviously not wanting to have this conversation.

"What?" I prod, with mock innocence. "You and Gabe have something special. It's about time you both admit it," I push. They should be together. They're perfect for one another and they're obviously both crazy about each other, but they've both been ignoring it for way too long.

"Gabe is my friend," she declares, defiantly. "That's it," she emphasizes, denying their connection.

I roll my eyes dramatically and slap my hand down on the counter. "Yeah and I'm leaving tomorrow to be a rodeo clown," I mutter, sarcastically.

"I'm surprised you like clowns, since you're a Stephen King fan," Ethan murmurs from behind me, startling me with his presence.

"Ethan!" I gasp, bringing my hand to my chest.

He smirks and takes a step towards me, my heart still racing. "Oh, so you do know my first name," he jokes.

I pinch my lips together and attempt to ignore his comment. I take a deep breath and clear my throat to calm myself down before I speak. Then I square my shoulders and sardonically reveal, "This is the kitchen, not the dining room."

He nods in acknowledgement, still grinning wide. "Yeah, but I heard voices. I figured you were talking to your sister," he informs me.

Hope grins and turns towards him without stepping away from the stove. "That's right. I'm Hope," she proclaims, introducing herself.

"Nice to meet you," he replies, returning her smile. "Ethan Dulane."

Hope turns back towards the stove and Ethan's plate. "Mr. Dulane is from New York City," I elaborate.

"Well, technically, I'm from Colorado," he corrects.

Hope freezes, still tightly gripping the spatula. She spins around and faces us, with her mouth hanging open and her eyes suddenly wide in shock. She gasps and brings her empty hand to her chest. "What?" I inquire, confused by her reaction.

She glances at me, with pure excitement lighting up her face. She bounces on her toes and gestures towards him as she exclaims, "Ethan Dulane! Oh my goodness. The Ethan Dulane!" she repeats, emphasizing each word as she steps closer to him.

"What are you talking about?" I prompt.

"I've read all your books," she enlightens him, ignoring my question. She looks up at him with sudden adoration, making my stomach flip with jealousy. "'Caribbean Sunset' was my favorite," she emphasizes.

I discount the feeling in my gut and smile, now understanding her excitement. I glance at Ethan and mumble, "Told you so."

He gives me a quick glance before focusing back on Hope. "Thank you," he tells her, appreciatively.

She sets the spatula down next to the sink and quickly strides around the counter. She closes the distance between them and reaches for his hand, shaking it enthusiastically. "It is such an honor to meet you," she announces, emphasizing each word. "Your books are amazing," she compliments him. "I feel like I'm everywhere that you write about. 'Paris in Love' was incredible. I could feel the rain under the Eiffel Tower," she praises, practically glowing as if it were her own memory and causing my whole body to tense.

"Oh, you've been to Paris?" Ethan inquires.

"Hope hasn't been anywhere," I interrupt, irritably.

Hope glares at me and I roll my eyes dramatically in response. She turns back to Ethan and continues. "No, but your description made me feel like I was there," she explains. "Please, sit," she encourages. "Let me get you dinner," she offers. The sudden way she's catering to him causes a lump to form in my throat.

Ethan smiles broadly and looks at me as he lowers himself onto the stool next to me. My insides continue to twist and I roll my eyes again, hating my reaction. "Wow, thank you so much," he murmurs, appreciatively.

"What would you like to drink?" she questions.

"What do you have?" he prompts.

"I made some apple cider this morning, if you'd like to try it," she suggests.

His eyes widen in surprise. "That sounds wonderful," he admits.

I watch as Hope rushes around the kitchen to wait on him. She hurries to grab the pitcher from the refrigerator and pours him a glass of cider.

"Can I have some too?" I ask, bitterly.

"Sure," she replies. She sets the pitcher on the counter and brings Ethan the full glass of cider she just poured. She places it in front of him, grinning, while she leaves me to fend for myself. I glare at her back before pouring my own glass of cider. She turns around and grabs the plate she just put together for him and brings it over, setting it in front of him.

"This looks delicious," he apprises.

"It's rosemary chicken and garlic potatoes," she informs him. "Is that okay?" she questions, anxiously. Hope never gets nervous.

"Yes, it's great," he confirms. "Thank you."

Hope stands watching him, grinning wide in complete awe. Ethan takes a bite of chicken and chews. "Do you like it?" she prompts.

He glances at her and nods his head in confirmation, attempting to finish chewing before he answers. "Yes. It's very good. Thank you," he replies.

She leans down and puts her elbows on the counter and places her chin in her hands. Then she smiles dreamily up at him, while he eats. "So what are you working on now?" she inquires.

I quickly gulp down my cider and stalk around the counter. I put my glass in the sink, annoyed with Hope. Of course the one guy I'm actually interested in, she's flirting with. I huff in irritation. "Good night, you two," I grumble.

"Where are you off to now?" Ethan probes, looking up at me from his seat.

"Out," I snap, testily. "Is that okay with you, Mr. Dulane?" I question, my voice thick with sarcasm.

"Joy!" Hope scolds, surprised at my retort. I glare at her and storm through the kitchen door, towards the dining area. I pause and take a deep breath to calm down as I storm away.

I hear Ethan's gravelly voice come through the door as he asks Hope, "What was that all about?"

"She might be feeling a little left out," Hope replies, making me even more annoyed. "She gets like that sometimes," she mumbles. I glare at her through the closed door, hurt by her response.

"Interesting," Ethan mumbles, thoughtfully.

My eyebrows draw down in confusion at his tone. What does he mean by that? I know I just met him, but I wish I knew what he thought of me. I grimace, at the same time not wanting to hear if they have anything bad to say about me. I huff and stalk through the empty dining room and front room, and storm into the lobby

"Joy," dad calls. I instantly stop in my tracks. I begrudgingly turn and face him, not able to hide my mood. "What's the matter?" he probes, his voice full of concern.

I step into the doorway and cross my arms over my chest. "Nothing," I grumble, defiantly.

He tilts his head and his eyebrows arch in challenge at the same time he appears to be fighting a smile. "Don't lie to me. It's written all over your face, Joy," he insists.

I sigh in exasperation and shake my head in disappointment. "I don't understand how a guy can come in here and in thirty seconds, Hope has him wrapped around her little finger," I spit out, bitterly.

Dad walks around the desk and puts his arm around me. "Honey," he begins, his tone soft, "I don't think that's the case," he claims, in attempt to comfort me.

"Yeah it is," I restate, as if it's fact. "She has something in common with everyone that steps onto the ranch," I claim.

He shakes his head in denial and tells me, "Nah, I don't think that's true."

"She talks to people so easily," I mutter.

"So do you," he contends.

I grimace. "Not really," I murmur.

"Stop comparing yourself to your sister, Joy," he demands. "You are two very different women," he reminds me.

"I know, I know," I mumble. Both our mom and our dad have told us over and over again to embrace our differences. That's what makes us both so special to them, but parents always say those kinds of things to their kids. I am proud of who I am, but it still hurts when she seems to get everything.

He arches his eyebrow in challenge. He prods, "Do you?"

I look up at my dad and sigh in defeat. "Yeah, I do," I concede.

"Besides, your sister only has eyes for Gabriel," he asserts.

My eyes widen and I gasp in surprise, "Daddy!"

He gives me a knowing grin. "What?" he shrugs. "You think I don't see it?" he questions.

"You never said anything before," I remind him.

"Honey, it's not a father's place to play matchmaker. They'll find each other eventually," he proclaims.

"Do you really think so?" I ask, hopeful. I really believe they were meant for each other. I thought they'd be together by now.

"Absolutely," he answers, confidently. "Gabe looks at Hope, the same way I used to look at your mother," he reveals.

My heart clenches painfully and a lump forms in my throat. I let my head fall to my dad's shoulder and lean into his chest, needing his support as sadness washes over me again. "I miss her, Daddy," I whisper, barely able to get the words out. Pain claws its way up my throat and an unwanted tear slips out.

He pulls me a little tighter and strokes the top of my head and down my hair, over and over, comforting both of us. "So do I, Joy. So do I," he murmurs, sadly.

Chapter 11

Hope

I pause and take a deep breath of the crisp morning air. I look around me, enjoying the sparkle of the sunlight as it spreads out over the ranch. A nice quiet morning like this is exactly what I needed after the night I had. I just wish I could sleep through the night for once without waking up to one of my nightmares. I can't keep reliving that day over and over again if I ever want to get past it. I'm just not sure how to do that. I take another deep breath, forcing the memories out of my head and trying to feel the calm. I shake my head and mutter, "I might as well keep on moving."

I walk over to the box of Christmas decorations, my cowboy boots kicking up the dust on the ground. I bend over and reach for another large red bow, to put on the outside of the gate. I stand up and tuck my hair behind my ear. I left it down today to keep me a little warmer, although I'm still dressed in layers. I have on fitted, dark blue jeans, a long-sleeved gray t-shirt, with a dark blue and gray flannel over top and my light blue jean jacket over that. I stride over to the fence and lean over, making sure to get every piece of the bow and tie on the outside of the fence. I don't want the horses to try to eat any of them and get sick.

"Good morning, Hope" Gabe calls.

I look up and meet his gaze. My heart instantly warms at the sight of Gabe, smiling at me, as he approaches. He's in his normal jeans and tan work boots with a gray thermal and a puffy, navy blue vest over it. "Morning, Gabe," I reply, returning his smile.

"Everything looks great," he praises me.

"You think?" I question.

He nods his head in affirmation as he looks around us, even though this is only a small part of the ranch. "Yeah," he confirms, a small smile on his face. "Really festive," he adds, gesturing towards the bows along the outside of the fence.

"Thanks," I murmur. I give him an appreciative smile, as I finish attaching the bow onto the outside of the fence. "We've got a lot to do," I remind him. We have a huge property and I like everything to be as cheerful as possible this time of year, at the same time, keeping the horses safe. I look back at him and request, "Would you mind hanging the large wreath above the stable doors for me?"

"Of course," he instantly agrees, with a nod of his head. He glances at his watch, before looking back up at me with his jaw suddenly tight. "Let me guess," he begins. "You've been here since five?" he prompts.

I wince and admit, "Five-thirty."

He gives me a look, making me blush. "It's eight," he states.

"And?" I question, defiantly.

He grimaces at my response. Then he questions, "You've been working on this for two and a half hours?"

"No, of course not," I reply, as I shake my head in denial. "It took me an hour to get the horses ready for the day," I inform him, gesturing towards the stables. I know that's not what he means, but I'm going to try anyway.

He heaves a sigh and stares at me as if he can read my mind. "Hope, what's going on with you?" he inquires, his green eyes full of concern.

My heart sinks and my shoulders sag, as I drop my head in defeat. I've been trying to hide it, but it's tough, especially when it comes to trying to hide something from Gabe. All I really want to do is share everything with him. Sometimes, it's just easier to pretend. "I don't want to talk about it," I insist, my tone haunted. I glance down at the ground, hoping he'll drop it, but I'm not that lucky.

He takes a step towards me, his face showing his worry. "You're not sleeping again?" he prompts. He gives me a look, as if he already knows the answer.

I turn away from him. Maybe if he doesn't see my face, he won't be able to read me. I pick up another bow for something to do and begin fidgeting with the tie attached to it. "Come on, Gabe," I plead, ignoring his question. "This ranch isn't going to decorate itself," I announce, as my weak attempt to change the subject.

I feel him reach out for me, even before I feel his touch. He gently grabs my arm and tugs me towards him, causing my heart to jump up to my throat and goosebumps to spread like wildfire over my whole body. "Come here," he encourages.

He wraps his arms around me. I resist at first, but I know his embrace is exactly where I want to be. I release a shuddering breath and melt into his chest. I wrap my arms around his waist and hold on tight. I heave a sigh, reveling in his comfort and the feeling of being safe, loved and protected. "The holidays are really hard, Gabe," I concede, my voice barely a hoarse whisper.

"I know," he acknowledges, squeezing me tighter.

I take a deep breath, breathing in his familiar scent of soap and the ranch, calming me even more. "I'm tired of people telling me how long it's been and that I should remember her and be happy," I confess. No one should tell me how to feel. I was the one that was there. They don't understand what I've been going through and what I see in my dreams every night when I close my eyes.

"I know," he repeats, his acknowledgement comforting. He continues rubbing his hands gently up and down my back, attempting to console me. He rests his head gently on top of mine, pulling me even closer.

"I miss her so much," I rasp. My chest aches painfully and I bury myself in Gabe's chest for support. My eyes well up and a few tears spill over onto my cheeks.

"I do, too," he agrees. His warm breath brushes over the top of my head, like a soothing blanket. A lump forms in my throat at his admission, causing me to squeeze him even tighter. I don't ever want to let go.

"Hey, you two!" Joy calls out. She strides towards the stables with Ethan in tow and a broad smile on her face. "About time!" she announces, happily.

I reflexively pull away from Gabe and he reluctantly releases me with a soft sigh. I quickly turn my back to all of them and take a deep breath. I discreetly try to wipe away my tears, without them seeing what a complete and utter mess I am.

Gabe glances at them and gives me one last look of empathy, before he quickly approaches them, protectively blocking me from their view as much as possible. He steps up to the latched gate and greets them. Like always, he's watching out for me, trying to give me some time to pull myself together. I gulp down the lump in my throat and admit to myself that I'm incredibly grateful for it and for him. I don't know what I'd ever do without him. It's times like this that I wish he saw us differently. "Morning, Joy," Gabe mumbles, finally responding to her greeting.

I hear the clanking sound of the gate bumping the latch, as they meet in the middle. "Gabe, this is Ethan Dulane," Joy announces, introducing the two men.

"Ethan, it's nice to meet you," Gabe states. He reaches over the gate towards Ethan, holding his hand out to shake.

"Pleasure," Ethan declares, as he shakes Gabe's hand. "Joy told me all about you at breakfast," he proclaims.

Gabe grins. "All good, I hope," he replies. He releases Ethan's hand and takes a small step away from the gate and towards me.

Joy throws her head back and laughs. "Hardly!" she claims, teasing Gabe. I turn around slowly and step up behind Gabe, as if he's my shield. I know I don't need him to protect me from my sister, but it helps anyway.

"Nah that's not true," Ethan insists, with a shake of his head. "She said you're like a brother," he explains.

My gaze snaps over to Joy's and I can't help but give her a look from behind Gabe. She smirks and mumbles, "Well, to me anyway."

Thankfully, Gabe ignores my sister's comment and focuses back on Ethan. "You're up awfully early for a guy on vacation," he recognizes, changing the subject.

Ethan offers us a crooked smile and shrugs like it's no big deal. "It's not exactly a vacation," he replies.

Joy grins broadly, a mischievous glint in her eyes. "He's here for Inspiration," she announces, bouncing on her toes in anticipation.

"Really?" Gabe questions. "I'm surprised a city slicker like you even heard of Inspiration," he mumbles. He glances at Ethan, slightly puzzled.

Ethan startles and his eyebrows draw down in confusion. "What's that supposed to mean?" he demands, marginally offended.

Joy quickly blurts out, "Nothing!" defending Gabe and probably hoping we don't give her joke away. Then she turns to face Ethan and nods towards the stables in encouragement. "Come on, I'll bring you to Inspiration," she offers.

Gabe's eyes widen in disbelief and he prods, "Wearing that?" We all take a moment to look Ethan up and down. We assess his black designer jeans, some type of black shirt underneath and matching black loafers. He has a brown, casual, winter coat over top, but that is the only thing that he's wearing that fits here. While Joy is dressed in her stylish, fitted jeans, cowboy boots with intricate teal stitching, a charcoal turtleneck sweater and a navy, puffy vest. She always finds a way to be dressed appropriately for the ranch, but also be incredibly stylish. Her hair looks perfect as well, clipped back away from her face with a simple bobby pin and a few large, loose curls hanging down over her shoulders.

"What's wrong with what I'm wearing?" Ethan inquires. He appears even more lost, as he holds out his arms and glances down at himself in confusion.

I bite my lip, fighting my smile, knowing exactly what Joy's up to. "You're not going to let him ride in that, right?" I prod. I don't believe she would, but I have to make sure. He'd definitely end up hurt if he tried to ride in those shoes.

"No, of course not," she replies, adamantly, with a shake of her head. She smirks and wiggles her eyebrows as she reaffirms, "But he asked for inspiration, so that's what he's going to get."

Joy and I both burst out laughing, not able to stop it from popping out. Gabe glances over at me and shakes his head in amusement, finally catching on. I glance up at Ethan, as I catch my breath. I can't help but feel a little bad for all his bewilderment, but Joy will straighten him out soon enough. Plus, she's definitely enjoying teasing him. Who am I to spoil her fun?

Ethan looks back and forth between all three of us, searching for some kind of hint as to what's happening. "What's going on?" he probes, anxiously.

Joy grins and responds playfully, announcing, "Come on, Mr. Dulane. I'll bring you to Inspiration." She unlatches the gate and pulls it open before she steps through, Ethan following right behind her. Then she immediately closes and locks the gate behind them, before she turns and saunters confidently towards the stables alongside Ethan.

As Gabe and I watch them walk away, Gabe glances at me and grins. "He has no idea what he's in for," he mumbles.

"Not a clue," I concur, giggling.

He chuckles and gives a light shake of his head. Then he brings his attention back over to me and his eyes immediately soften, causing my heart to skip a beat. "There it is," he mumbles, under is breath, the corners of his mouth curving upwards. "I love to see you happy," he quietly confesses. "You have a beautiful smile, Hope," he praises. I feel my cheeks heat with his compliment. I keep smiling, but turn away, hiding my blush. I make my way back to the box of Christmas decorations, with Gabe following right behind me.

I pick up the large wreath and hand it to him. He grips it, but stops me from turning back around. "Hey, Hope," he prompts.

"Yes?" I rasp.

He looks into my eyes and emphasizes, "I'm right here when you're ready to talk about it. You need to talk about it."

I pinch my lips tightly together and give him a stiff nod of my head in acknowledgement. I let go of the wreath and question, "Do you want me to hold the ladder for you?"

He shakes his head in response and mumbles, "Nah, you can keep doing the bows. I can get Eddie to help me," he reveals.

"Okay, thank you," I reply.

Chapter 12

Ethan

I follow Joy into the stables, my stomach twisting as she looks back at me with a flirtatious smile. She steps up to one of the individual stables and makes a clicking sound with her mouth two times. Then she pulls a peppermint out of her back pocket and holds it out with her hand flat. A beautiful chestnut colored horse with a jagged white stripe on it's nose, sticks his nose out towards her, causing me to reflexively take a step back.

"Whoa!" I gasp, with wide eyes. The horse is a lot bigger than I anticipated. Then again, I'm not really sure what I expected.

Joy turns and smirks at me, as the horse eats the peppermint right out of her hand. "What's the matter? Never seen a horse before?" she challenges, playfully.

I huff a nervous laugh and shrug my shoulders. "Sure I have," I mutter, "just not in person." The corners of my own mouth twitch up as I begin to relax, just watching her run her hand lovingly along the horse's long neck.

"Really?" she prompts, surprised. "You've never ridden a horse?" she reiterates, obviously needing clarification.

"Does a carousel count?" I question, jokingly.

She laughs, while rubbing Charley's nose, the light sound causing my heart to skip a beat. "So what in the

97

world are you doing at a horse ranch?" she inquires, sounding bewildered.

I shrug my shoulders and answer honestly, "Like I said, my publisher thought I could find some inspiration up here."

She grins wide, a mischievous glint in her eyes that I'm really starting to enjoy. She happily announces, "Here he is!" Then she glances at the horse, continuing to pet him, before glancing expectantly back at me.

I look back and forth between her and the horse, attempting to understand what she means. This horse is supposed to help me come up with a story and write my book? I grimace and look at Joy with a question in my eyes. "I don't get it," I grumble.

"Ethan Dulane," she begins, with her eyes focused momentarily on me. Then she turns back to the horse and finally elaborates, "Meet Charlene's Inspiration, also known as Charley."

My eyes widen in shock, realizing she's been playing me this whole time. "You're kidding!" I mutter and chuckle softly under my breath. "The horse's name is Inspiration?" I clarify.

"It sure is!" she proclaims, smiling brightly. "Look," she encourages. She points to a wooden plaque mounted just above the horse's stable, reading, "Charlene's Inspiration," in beautiful gold lettering.

I gesture towards the plaque and prompt, "Who is Charlene?"

"My grandma," Joy replies.

"In Florida, right?" I prod.

She grins, proudly as she looks at me. "Right," she confirms. "You listened. I'm impressed," she proclaims.

"I'm a good listener," I tell her, truthfully. As a writer, I tend to listen to what's going on and take in details of my surroundings, but there's also something about Joy that makes me want to sit up and really pay attention.

"Are you a good student, too?" she inquires, a teasing tone in her voice.

"It depends on what I'm learning," I admit.

"I can teach you how to ride," she offers.

"Ride?" I question, with wide eyes. "A horse?" I clarify, suddenly nervous at the idea of climbing up on a horse even if it is the best thing to do for my book.

She rolls her eyes and answers me with obvious sarcasm, "No, a bike." She shakes her head and giggles. "Of course, a horse!" she states, emphatically.

"Yeah...Um, I...I don't know about that," I stammer, anxiously.

She pops her hip out and plants her hand on her hip as she smirks up at me. "Ethan Dulane, you are staying on a horse ranch," she reminds me of the obvious. "Don't you think you should take Inspiration by the reigns?" she teases me.

"Maybe not quite so literally!" I exclaim. I gesture to the horse, finally understanding her joke.

She turns away from the horse and looks me in the eyes. "Look," she begins softly, "I'll start you on a smaller horse," she suggests. "Okay," she prompts.

I breathe a sigh of relief, feeling a sense of comfort wash over me as I look into those gorgeous blue eyes. Then I tilt my head to the side and question, "You wont think I'm a baby?" I watch her intently for her reaction.

"Oh, I already think you're a baby," she taunts.

"Come on!" I mutter, even though I know she's teasing me. The corners of my mouth twitch up in amusement despite myself.

She takes a step towards me and stops. She looks up into my eyes, her own blue eyes sparkling with encouragement. "We'll start you out slow, okay?" she prods. "Not everyone has the opportunity to ride horses," she reminds me. She glances back at the horse and murmurs reverently, "By the time you leave, you'll be in love."

My eyes widen in surprise and the corners of my mouth curve upwards without my consent. "Excuse me?" I blurt out.

Her eyes widen and she opens and closes her mouth like a fish the moment she realizes her mistake. She instantly turns a beautiful deep shade of red and spins away from me. "With the horses. I meant the horses," she stammers.

I chuckle softly, enjoying our banter. "Sure you did," I murmur, playfully, finally feeling like I've gotten some of my footing back.

She takes a deep breath before looking back at me, obviously fighting a smile. "Stop" she requests. "Lets get you some real riding gear," she proposes, effectively changing the subject.

"What's wrong with what I'm wearing?" I repeat the same question I asked earlier. I glance down at my clothes again.

She looks me up and down and smirks. "You look like you're going to read poems at the bookstore," she informs me.

"There's nothing wrong with that," I claim, slightly defensive. "What if I like reading poems at a bookstore?" I challenge.

"You'll find one in town. Open mic night is Thursday," she enlightens me, without judgment.

"Okay, okay," I relent, finally comprehending that it's not about my taste in clothes. "What do I need to wear?" I probe.

"Do you have blue jeans?" she questions.

"Sure," I reply, nodding my head in confirmation.

"And you'll want to layer up," she recommends. "Like a t-shirt and a sweater under your jacket," she adds.

"One step ahead of you," I tell her, with a proud grin. I unzip my jacket, revealing a charcoal zip sweater over a black t-shirt.

"Okay," she concedes. "But your shoes," she grimaces as she looks at my feet. "You can't wear loafers on a horse," she proclaims.

"Why not?" I prod.

"They're not sturdy enough," she insists. "You can get hurt and you won't be able to control the horse as well," she notifies me. "Do you have boots?" she inquires.

"I brought snow boots," I confirm.

She gives me a look as if I've lost my mind. Then she shakes her head in disbelief and heaves a heavy sigh. "Time to go to town, Ethan. You need to buy a pair of boots," she announces.

I glance at my watch, realizing it's not quite 8:30am. I inquire, "Are they open now?"

She shakes her head, "Not until nine. If we walk though, I can show you around," she offers, with a quick glance in my direction.

"Now walking is something I can do," I joke, grinning at her.

She giggles, appreciating my humor. "Follow me, Mr. Dulane," she instructs. Then she spins on her heel and starts to walk away. I glance at Charley one more time, before I turn around and jog a few steps to catch up with Joy, following her across the ranch.

As we walk through the ranch, she points out a few more areas with stables housing other horses and corrals for the horses to run. They even have an indoor riding ring and trails all over the property. This ranch is bigger than I imagined and it really is incredible. They have several different areas for the horses, spread out in a U shape around the Inn and their family home. Then beyond that they have fields where they harvest hay for the horses and a few gardens, with trails all over the property for them to ride the horses and take guests on. I imagine some of the views on those rides are spectacular. We walk on the grass next to the street with a fence on our left. "Is this still your property?" I question.

She nods in confirmation. "Yes, we have almost 500 acres, but most of it goes back that way, she points beyond the fence, "and then that way," she adds, gesturing behind us, where we just came from.

"I'm surprised there aren't any sidewalks here," I murmur, thoughtfully.

She shrugs, as if it's no big deal. "We don't need sidewalks out here. There's not that much traffic," she states. "There are sidewalks in town," she adds.

"How far is town?" I inquire.

"A little over a mile," she enlightens me.

I arch my eyebrows in surprise and probe, "A mile? Really?" It feels like we're so much further out when I look around and see nothing but open space.

"Is that too far for you?" she challenges.

I chuckle softly and shake my head. "No, not at all. I run marathons," I tell her.

"I only run when I'm chased," she proclaims, playfully.

My chest tightens and I murmur, "I'll keep that in mind." I take a deep breath and continue. "I don't keep a car in the city, so I try to walk everywhere." I shrug and add, "Besides, it's easier if you walk in the city."

She nods her head in acknowledgment. "I like walking when the weather is like this. Chilly, but not cold," she explains. She takes a deep breath, inhaling deeply with a small smile on her face. "You can smell the fireplaces and the leaves. Sometimes, when it's really cold you can even smell the snow."

"Really?" I prompt, not able to take my eyes off of her.

"Yeah," she nods in confirmation. "You just know that snow is coming by the way the air smells," she informs me, wistfully.

"I've never heard that before," I reveal.

She glances at me, the corners of her mouth tugging upward in amusement. "I'm sure you're going to hear a lot of things that you've never heard before while you're up here," she claims, making me chuckle. She's probably right.

I grin down at her feeling inspired just walking next to this beautiful, smart and feisty woman. "I suddenly feel my creativity unblocking," I confess.

She smirks and arches her eyebrows in challenge. "I thought you said you didn't have writer's block," she reminds me.

I flinch, hating those words. I give her a look as if in warning and a triumphant smile instantly engulfs her whole face, causing my stomach to flip-flop. I shake my head in amusement and she nudges me with her elbow.

We continue walking, soon finding ourselves on the quaint Main Street of Evergreen Valley, with one stoplight in the middle of town. Most of the stores are already decorated for the holidays with lights, greenery and window displays that would make the city proud. Wreaths with red ornaments and red bows are found on every lamppost and bench we pass by. Joy waves to a few people outside a hair salon still decorating the outside of the shop. They immediately brighten, returning her greeting and bringing a smile to my face. That's one of the things I love about small towns; everyone knows everyone and even if they didn't, they'd still be polite and welcome you with open arms. You don't find that in the city. She gestures to a shop on our left and announces, "Here we are."

I pull the door open and let her go in front of me. I step in behind her and let my eyes scan over the contents of the store. I spot a lot of jeans, flannel, large buckle belts, cowboy boots and hats. I'm definitely not in my element.

Chapter 13

Gabe

I rush into the inn and turn right, towards the front desk, knowing that's where I'll find Frank. "Mr. McGregor, you need to come outside," I encourage, urgently.

"What's the matter?" he questions.

I shake my head barely able to comprehend the situation myself. I insist, "You wouldn't believe me if I told you." I turn around and run back out to the circular drive in front of the inn, with Frank following right behind me. I can hear Hope yelling the moment I push through the front door.

"How am I supposed to explain this to everyone?" she challenges, Tommy. Her voice becomes unnaturally louder and higher with every word out of her mouth.

Tommy stands casually with one hand hanging at his side and the other, mindlessly running over the scruff along his jaw as he looks down at Hope with his blue-grey eyes. He shrugs his shoulders, like it's no big deal. Tommy's dressed in jeans, work boots, a blue-grey t-shirt and a gray and white, wool lined flannel jacket, with a gray hat pulled down over his shaggy, blonde hair. He shakes his head, dismissing any issue. "I don't know what to tell you, Hope," he mumbles and shrugs carelessly. It says four feet right here," he insists. He gives her a patronizing grin, as he points to the purchase order in his hand, as if they're his words to live by.

I step up next to Hope, hoping to support her and with any luck, keep her calm, while her dad goes to her other side. "I don't care what it says!" she exclaims. "Why would I place an order for a four foot tree a year in advance?" she questions, demanding an answer.

"What seems to be the problem here?" Frank interrupts. Hopefully, he'll be able to turn this situation around before Hope loses her mind.

Tommy turns to Mr. McGregor and greets him with a nod of his head. "Hi, Frank," he murmurs, politely.

"Tommy, where's your dad?" Frank inquires.

"He wanted me to run the business this year," he states as an answer. "You know, keeping it in the family or whatever," he grumbles, irritably.

Hope's eyes narrow to barely slits as she glares at him. "You did this on purpose!" she accuses.

"Calm down, Hope," I mumble, softly, in attempt to comfort her. I place my hand on her lower back in support.

"I will not calm down!" she proclaims, defiantly, with barely a glance in my direction.

"Well, Frank," Tommy begins, "it seems your daughter ordered the wrong size Christmas tree for the Two Sisters Tree Lighting," he announces, as the corners of his mouth twitch up in amusement. I grind my teeth in annoyance, but keep my mouth shut. It's not going to help Hope if I start screaming too.

"I did not!" Hope yells, defensively. "I ordered a forty-foot tree last year. The same way that we've done every year since mom and Aunt Faith started the tree lighting," she elaborates, her eyes narrowed on Tommy.

"Maybe so," Tommy shrugs again, "but it says right here 'four foot'," he reiterates, pointing to the purchase order again.

"Tommy, come on," Frank utters, with clear exasperation. "You know we get a forty foot tree every year," he reminds him.

"No," Tommy claims, shaking his head. "This is my first year with the business," he reiterates. "I never delivered your tree before," he clarifies, as if he's never even been to the annual tree lighting here before.

"Use some common sense!" Hope exclaims. "Do you see the cost?" she challenges, clearly frustrated for good reason.

"Eleven hundred dollars," he confirms, with a nod of his head.

"Exactly! Do you think that a four foot Christmas tree costs over a thousand dollars?" she probes, her face red with anger.

"What do I know?" he shrugs, feigning ignorance. "This is my..." he begins to repeat himself.

"First year in the business," Hope interrupts, finishing his statement. "I know," she grumbles, irritably.

"I hope you don't think we're paying eleven hundred dollars for a four foot Christmas tree, Son," Frank confronts him.

"That's what the purchase order says," Tommy reiterates.

Hope gasps again, as her eyes go wide and her mouth drops open in shock at his audacity. "Are you kidding me?" Hope screams. She flings her arms out and lunges at Tommy. I reflexively reach out and wrap my arm around her waist and pull her back tightly against my chest, trying to stop her from doing anything she might regret later. I only have about an inch on him, but he has a little broader frame than me. I don't want her to start something none of us want to finish, although I would for her. I'd do anything for her.

"Hope, chill out," I encourage, gently, but firm. I maintain my tight hold around her waist, keeping her close to my chest. I practically feel her anger radiating off of her.

"Take the tree, Tommy," Frank demands, leaving no room for argument. "We can get a bigger one for fifty bucks somewhere else," he insists.

Tommy shrugs like its no big deal to him, but this will devastate Hope if we don't figure it out. "Suit yourself," he grumbles. He turns and starts to drag the tree away. Then he suddenly stops and spins back around. He pastes a fake smile on his face before he requests, "Make sure you let my dad know how pleased you are with my service."

Hope attempts to lunge at him again, but I maintain my firm grip around her waist, holding her back against me.

"You can bet I will," Frank grumbles, his jaw tight.

"Thanks," Tommy replies, appreciatively, with a genuine smile lighting up his face. He waves and continues to drag the tree back to his truck.

Hope wiggles out of my arms, breaking away from my hold and storms off. She stalks around behind the inn heading towards the stables. "I'll talk to her," Frank offers.

I shake my head and insist, "No, I got it."

"You sure?" he prods.

"Yeah," I confirm, as I watch her storm away.

"Suit yourself," Frank mumbles. He turns and strides back towards the inn, while I hurry after Hope.

"Hope! Hope! Wait up!" I call out, jogging towards her.

She suddenly spins around and I stop in my tracks. "Can you believe that guy?" she questions, testily. "He ruined the tree lighting," she announces, sounding both stressed and hurt by the prospect.

"No, he didn't," I insist, shaking my head.

"Gabe, how are we supposed to have a tree lighting without a tree?" she questions, desperately.

"We can still get a tree," I claim.

"Not a big one!" she emphasizes, sounding defeated.

"Does it matter?" I prompt.

"Of course it does!" she exclaims, defiantly.

I shake my head sadly, knowing she just wants everything to be like it used to be before the accident and I would give it to her if I could. "Hope, no it doesn't," I assert. "The tree lighting isn't about the tree. It's about the holidays. It's about our community coming together to celebrate each other. It's about love," I emphasize. "The tree is just decoration," I remind her.

She pouts, sticking her lower lip out, just a little bit. I bite my lip, fighting my smile that wants to break through. I can't help it. She looks so adorable right now, but I know a grin would just get me in trouble. "But I love that decoration," she confesses, emphatically, causing me to sigh softly.

My heart clenches tightly, wishing I could do more. "Look," I begin. "I'll go over to Matt's Christmas Tree Farm and pick out the biggest Christmas tree that I can. We can put it up on some bales of hay to make it higher," I suggest. "We'll just decorate it even more than normal, okay?" I prompt, hoping it's enough to calm her anxiety.

"I...I don't know," she stammers, hesitant.

I encourage her, desperate to make her feel better. I offer, "You don't even have to go with me. I'll get it all by myself."

"No," she grimaces and shakes her head. "That's not it, Gabe. I'm just disappointed is all," she concedes, sadly.

I take a deep breath and exhale slowly, my insides aching with her admission. "I know you are," I murmur, with my heart full of regret. I look into her sad brown eyes and her sorrow almost tears me apart. I have to do everything I can to fix this. "I'll leave now, okay? I'll be back before sunset," I propose.

She sighs sadly and nods her head in acknowledgement. I turn and begin making my way towards my truck. "Gabe!" Hope calls out, stopping me in my tracks.

I spin back around and Hope slows her pace as she approaches me. I arch my eyebrow in question and prompt, "Yeah?"

"I..." she begins, then grimaces and pauses. She shakes her head slightly as if she's changing her mind about what she wants to say to me. Then she looks me in the eyes and offers me a small smile. "Make sure it's perfect, okay?" she requests. "Like a perfect triangle," she adds.

I grin down at her, feeling relief wash over me, knowing she's going to be okay. "Don't worry. I know what you like," I claim. Then I turn and stride towards my truck. I open the door and hop into the driver's seat. I put the key in the ignition and turn it, waiting for the low rumble. Then I buckle my seatbelt, before I glance behind me and put my truck into gear. I begin slowly backing out.

"Gabe! Gabe wait!" Hope yells, running towards me down the dirt drive.

My heart jumps into my throat, worried something is wrong. I slam on the brake and throw the truck back into park. I turn it off and jump out of the truck, rushing to her side. I put my hands gently on her arms, with the strongest desire to protect her. "What's the matter?" I prompt. My heart pounds so hard in fear, I feel as if it might burst out of my chest.

"I'll...I'll come," she stutters.

My mouth drops open, I gasp and my eyes widen in shock. "What?" I question, needing clarification.

"I'll come," she states, with a little more determination. "I want to come with you," she repeats, with even more confidence.

"You sure?" I prod, my skin beginning to tingle with anticipation.

"Yeah," she nods, "but let's go now before I change my mind," she urges, sounding almost frantic.

"Okay," I agree. I put my hand on her back and swiftly lead her around to the other side of my truck. I open the door and help her inside, before I close the door behind her. I quickly stride around the front of the truck and get back in behind the wheel. I buckle my seatbelt and start my truck back up. I glance over at Hope with her eyes squeezed shut,

111

concentrating on taking deep breaths in and out. She's gripping the handle of the door with a death grip, her knuckles turning white. While she might leave nail marks in the seat with her other one. But it's not the truck I care about. Hope can do anything she wants to this thing, as long as she's okay. "Are you okay?" I inquire, full of concern.

"Yup," she claims, without opening her eyes or even moving an inch.

"You sure?" I prompt, uneasily.

"Just drive, Gabe," she snaps, anxiously.

"Okay," I instantly agree. I put the truck in gear and back out of the driveway. I pull onto the road and turn towards Matt's Tree Farm, glancing over at Hope every chance I get. I need to make sure she's still with me every step of the way. I'm so proud of her. I need to make every minute of this trip worth it.

Chapter 14

Joy

I look down and let my hair fall over my face. I glance up at Ethan from underneath my eyelashes, as I walk next to him up the long driveway towards the inn. Then I look up ahead, as I notice Gabe slowly approaching in his pick-up truck. I step onto the grass, out of the way and stop, lifting my hand to wave to him. I suddenly freeze as he comes closer. My eyes narrow as I realize that someone is sitting next to him in the passenger seat and it appears to be a woman. I hold my breath, my whole body tense and continue to stare, anxiously waiting to see who's beside him. As he nears I notice long, wavy, brown hair and then her features swiftly become clear. She looks exactly like my sister, with her body taut and her eyes squeezed tightly shut. I gasp in shock and watch as Gabe pulls out of the driveway and onto the street, not even glancing in my direction. My mouth hangs open as I turn to look at Ethan with wide eyes and utter disbelief. "Was that my sister?" I question, my breath hitching in shock.

Ethan turns and looks after the truck. He's still carrying the shopping bags from our trip into town with all his new ranch clothes. "I don't know," he mumbles and shrugs his shoulders. "I didn't see," he admits.

I shake my head in disbelief and take a deep breath, momentarily overwhelmed. A small smile touches my lips, as I think about what this means. "I think it was!" I announce. I feel my excitement building up inside me.

I spin on my heel and take off in a sprint towards the inn to find my dad, without giving any explanation to a confused Ethan. "Joy?" he calls after me. "Joy!" he yells again, but I keep running. He'll catch up and I need to see my dad.

I burst through the front door of the inn and into the front office. "Dad! Dad!" I yell, my excitement practically rolling off me in waves.

The moment he sees the broad smile on my face, he rushes around the desk and wraps his arms around me, his own shining through. "Can you believe it?" he prompts, his grin mirroring mine.

"It was really her?" I probe, still struggling to believe the truth.

He pulls back and lets his hands rest on my shoulders, as he looks me in the eyes. He nods his head in confirmation, fighting back tears. His Adam's apple bobs up and down as he swallows hard before he proudly confirms, "It was."

I feel Ethan walk into the room behind me. Then a sudden flash of worry bursts through me as I run through her possible reasons for leaving the ranch. My eyebrows draw down in trepidation and I question, "Did she get hurt or something?"

"Is everything okay?" Ethan inquires, his tone full of concern.

Dad instantly eases my fears as his smile broadens and he brushes the tears from the corners of his eyes. "It's better than okay," he affirms. He glances at Ethan and then back at me as he reiterates what we already know, "Hope left the ranch."

We hug again in pure joy and relief. "I can't believe it!" I repeat in awe.

Dad shakes his head and concurs, "Neither can I."

"I don't follow," Ethan murmurs. He looks back and forth between my dad and me, obviously a little lost without the rest of the story.

I let go of my dad and turn to face Ethan. "You wouldn't," I acknowledge. "It's a long story," I inform him, not able to wipe the smile off my face.

Ethan purses his lips and shrugs his shoulders, as if listening to me isn't a big deal. Then he reminds me, "I like stories and I've got plenty of time."

I glance back at my dad for approval to tell our story and how it affected Hope. It affected all of us, but Hope more than anyone with how everything occurred. He nods his head in encouragement. "Go on and tell him," he agrees. Then he looks at Ethan and suggests, "You might want a glass of wine with it."

I bounce on my toes and joke, "Or champagne." My dad smiles in response. I spin back around and face Ethan. "Go put your stuff away and meet me in the kitchen, Ethan. Okay?" I request, making sure that works for him. He smiles and nods in agreement. "Do you like wine?" I inquire.

"Sure," he easily agrees.

"Red or white?" I ask, for clarification.

"Surprise me," he replies, with a grin.

I nod and Ethan turns to leave, heading up the stairs to his room. I step back towards my dad and throw my arms around him one more time. For the first time in a really long time, everything finally feels like it's coming together. I release him and head for the kitchen, practically dancing all the way there. I'm barely able to contain my excitement. Maybe this means other things will start to turn around for her too. It's about time she and Gabe figure out what's between them. I heave a happy sigh, smiling to myself, as I pull out a bottle of white wine and two wine glasses. I pour wine into both glasses and then sit down at the end of the counter to wait for Ethan. I sip my wine and smile to myself as I think about Hope finally leaving the ranch. Mom would be so proud of her.

I have the same bright blue eyes and blonde hair as my mom. I have her build too, but I have my dad's height. She was an incredibly smart and kind woman. She always wanted to do what she could to help everyone else, especially when it came to family. Family always came first. Then there's Aunt Faith. She was not only my mom's sister, but she was also her best friend. She treated Hope and me as if we were her own. Plus, Hope looked a lot like her with her brown hair and eyes and more petite build. We were all obviously devastated when we lost both of them so tragically at the same time, but we all dealt with it much differently. Then again, the day it happened was completely different for each of us.

I take another sip of my wine and close my eyes. I take a deep breath, steeling myself, as I prepare to tell Ethan the story. I've never really told anyone this story before. Everyone around here just seemed to know or at least know enough to not ask questions, but I want Ethan to know because I'd like him to really know me. I open my eyes just as he enters the kitchen, my heart skipping a beat. I look up at him and smile as he lowers himself onto the stool next to me at the counter. I wordlessly hand him the glass of wine and then hold my own up towards him. "Cheers," I toast.

He grins and holds his glass up to me, repeating, "Cheers."

We gently clink glasses and we both take a sip before I return my glass to the counter. I look up at him, hesitantly. "Are you sure you want to hear this story?" I clarify.

He smiles sadly and nods in confirmation. "Absolutely. I mean, it clearly affected you and your dad," he assesses.

I heave a sigh and concede, "You have no idea."

"I'm listening," he voices in encouragement.

I start fidgeting with the stem of my wine glass as I speak, needing to do something with my hands. "Almost five years ago, my mom and aunt were killed in a really bad car accident," I begin.

He nods in acknowledgement and offers me an empathetic smile. "Yeah, you said so last night," he reminds me.

I nod my head in acknowledgement and continue. "Hope was almost in the car," I blurt out.

His eyebrows draw down in confusion. "Almost?" he prompts. "What do you mean?" he quesitons for clarification.

"Hope and Mom were out riding on the trails," I enlighten him. "They would ride the trails every day. Mom would ride Charley and Hope would ride Westie," I reveal.

"I haven't met Westie yet," he comments.

"You will," I insist. "He's Hope's horse," I add.

"Go on," he encourages me.

"From what Hope told me, her and mom were having a great time, until Aunt Faith called," I explain.

"Why?" he inquires. "What happened?"

"My dad fell through the barn roof. Gabe saw the whole thing. He stayed back with my dad while Aunt Faith called the ambulance and then my mom," I describe, attempting to keep my emotions at bay.

"Is that why he limps?" he probes.

"Yeah," I concur. "He was hurt really bad. Mom told Aunt Faith where she and Hope were, so she could pick her up and bring her to the hospital."

"What about Hope?" he prods.

"She planned on going to the hospital with Gabe after bringing the horses back to the stables," I explain.

He nods in understanding, "Oh, okay."

"Well, Aunt Faith picked mom up. She turned around so she was headed towards the hospital. She stopped about 20 yards from where Hope was standing," I describe, envisioning the scene in front of me. I gulp down the growing lump in my throat and continue. "Someone blew the stop sign at the intersection and hit mom and Aunt Faith."

I hear his quick intake of breath as his eyes widen in shock. He probes, "Right in front of your sister?"

I gulp and nod sadly, feeling as if my heart suddenly weighs me down. "Right in front of my sister," I confirm. I take another sip of wine to calm myself down before I continue. "Everyone in the crash was killed. Hope was the one that called the ambulance. Charley and Westie took off running toward the ranch," I inform him.

"What happened next?" he questions.

"Well," I begin, "Gabe was in the stables waiting for them to come back and saw the horses without mom and Hope, so he knew something was wrong. He hopped in his car and took off. Got there at the same time as the ambulance," I reveal and grimace.

"Where were you?" he asks.

"College, down in New Jersey. I got the call a few hours later," I reply, bitterly, as my stomach twists at the memory. I still hate that I wasn't here with my family when it happened, or that I had to hear about it over the phone. I'll never forget that phone call or the hollow sound of Gabe's voice when he told me what happened. I barely remember making it home.

"I'm so sorry," Ethan responds, sympathetically.

I lift my wine glass to my lips and take a large gulp before replying. "Thanks," I mumble. "Anyway," I sigh and continue. "When Hope got back from the funeral, she wouldn't leave her room for nearly two weeks."

"Really?" he asks.

I nod in confirmation, "Yeah. She would only talk to me, dad or Gabe. She wouldn't take any visitors. She just pulled back into this shell," I tell him, attempting to describe the situation the best way I can.

His eyes widen as understanding dawns on him and he nods his head. "Oh," he mumbles, drawing out the word. "She wouldn't leave the ranch."

I offer him a sad smile and confirm, "Exactly." I pause and look into his eyes, wanting him to see the effect Hope leaving the ranch today has truly had on me. "Today was the first time in nearly five years that my sister has stepped foot off the ranch," I reveal, feeling raw and vulnerable.

"Not even to ride?" he questions, obviously surprised.

I wince and shake my head sadly. "My sister hasn't ridden a horse since that day," I admit.

"Really?" he prods, his eyes rounding even wider.

I wince and concede, "Yeah. She'll tack them, she'll groom them, she'll even walk them out, but I haven't seen her in a saddle in years. Not since before I left for college that year," I inform him.

"That's so sad," he concurs.

I flinch, agreeing with his statement and heave a heavy sigh. "Well, that's the ballad of Hope McGregor," I grumble.

He takes a sip of wine, pondering my story. Then he looks at me and states, "Well, it seems like the tune is changing, don't you think?" he prompts, attempting to make me feel better.

I bite my lower lip and slowly release it. "I sure hope so," I admit. I take another sip of my wine, before setting my glass down in front of me and turning to look at him, assessing his reaction of everything I just unloaded on him. I have to admit, he made it incredibly easy for me to tell him all of this. Hopefully my tragic story doesn't push him away. I don't want it to. I haven't wanted someone to stick around in a very long time, but with Ethan, I really don't want to scare him away. I want to share things with him instead.

"Thank you for sharing that story with me, Joy. I realize it wasn't easy for you," he acknowledges. I look into his eyes and don't see anything, but empathy in them. I offer him a small smile in response. It may not be easy, but he definitely made it easier for me to tell it for the first time just looking into the comfort of his warm hazel eyes.

Chapter 15

Gabe

The gravel crunches under my tires as I pull into the parking lot at Matt's Tree Farm. I park my truck and turn the ignition off. I glance at Hope and a small smile plays on my lips, while a rush of warmth spreads throughout my body at the sight of her sitting beside me. She still has her eyes shut tight and she's focusing on breathing in and out. I watch as her chest rises and then falls as she slowly exhales. I'm so proud of her. I force myself to look away and hop out of the truck. I quickly stride around to the other side and pull the passenger door open. "Hope, we're here," I announce, gently. She remains still, except for her deep breathing, causing my concern to take over. I lean in towards her and place my hand softly on her shoulder. I gently prod, "Hope. Are you okay?"

She exhales again and then slowly opens her eyes and nods her head. She unbuckles her seat belt and then finally looks me in the eyes. "Yeah," she grins. "I'm good," she confirms.

I breathe a sigh of relief, wanting to kiss her, but I hold myself back and return her smile instead. She holds onto my arm as I attempt to help her out of my truck. "You sure?" I prompt, needing more reassurance of my own.

She offers me her sweet smile as her feet hit the grass. Then she reiterates, "Yeah. Mind if I hold onto you?" she requests.

"Nope," I tell her. My heart instantly picks up its pace in response. "That's fine," I agree, attempting to keep my tone casual. It's more than fine, but I don't want to make her uncomfortable. Right now, this is about her. I'm so proud of her for taking this step and I don't want anything to stand in her way, especially me. I'm thrilled I get to be the one to be here for her and that's enough for me, right now.

She wraps her hand around my forearm and holds on tight as we walk in the dirt towards the Christmas trees, the scent of pine suddenly overwhelming. We walk by a young couple, talking animatedly about buying their first Christmas tree as we begin to stroll through paths of mostly stumps, with so many of the trees already sold. We finally come to several paths where all the Christmas trees on both sides of us, stand about the same height as Hope and some even a little shorter. Unfortunately, all the trees are almost all picked over this close to Christmas and most of the ones remaining are either thin, not very tall or something else is wrong with it that I know Hope won't like. I begin commenting on different trees to assess her reaction. "This one looks good," I murmur.

Hope grimaces and shakes her head. "No, there's too many pinecones," she states. I immediately realize she's right. I've honestly never seen so many pinecones on a Christmas tree before.

I saunter towards another tree and inquire, "This one?"

She replies almost instantly, "Too short."

We keep walking and I spot an extremely small tree with sparse pine needles. I smirk in amusement of what I'm about to suggest. "This one?" I question, already knowing the answer.

She arches her eyebrows and looks up at me from underneath her eyelashes, telling me it's not the time to joke. Then she warns, "Don't."

We approach another one and I step towards the tree, holding my hand out. I suggest, "What about this one?" She lets go of my arm and steps closer to the tree to get a better look. "It's a good size," I claim.

She steps around it and then grimaces and shakes her head in refusal. "There's a big hole in it," she declares.

I don't want to give her a hard time, but she's going to have to settle for something this year, or I'm not going to be able to help. "Hope, you're being too picky," I complain.

"No, I'm not," she argues, shaking her head in denial. "This is the first time in years that we aren't having a huge tree," she reminds me, as if I've already forgotten. "It needs to be perfect," she insists, vehemently.

A man steps up to us, interrupting our conversation. "Hey! You folks need help?" he offers.

I turn to face him and meet friendly blue eyes. I instantly recognize my old friend, with his red hair peaking out from underneath a dark blue hat and matching, neatly trimmed, red beard. He's wearing dark blue jeans and dark brown work boots, a grey t-shirt with a grey and green flannel over the top and his dark blue and grey winter coat, unzipped. "Matt!" I exclaim. "Hey," I greet him with a wide smile.

He startles slightly at my friendly greeting and does a double take. His eyes suddenly widen in recognition and he questions, "Gabe?" He steps closer and inquires, "Gabriel Corsetti?"

123

"In the flesh," I announce. I hold my arms out, as a broad smile lights up my face.

"Wow! It's so good to see you!" he states, grinning. He holds his coffee cup out to the side as we step towards one another and exchange a friendly hug, with a hard pat on the back.

"What are you doing here?" I question, as I take a step back. "I thought you were out in California," I tell him.

He nods his head in agreement. "I was, I was," he stammers and crosses his arms across his chest. "Came back when dad had the heart attack," he informs me, matter of fact.

I wince and nod my head in acknowledgement. "Yeah, I heard about that," I murmur. "How's he doing now?" I prompt.

"Good! He's good," he reiterates. "Mom's making him rest and he's going a little stir crazy," he admits, with a shrug.

"I can imagine," I concede.

"Well, you know, since he named the farm after me, I figured I should at least come help him for the holidays," he explains, "you know?"

I nod in understanding, "Yeah, absolutely."

Matt looks towards Hope, who's wandered slightly away from me to look at the trees. Then he focuses back on me with a curious look in his eyes. "Is that Hope McGregor?" he whispers.

"Yeah," I proudly, declare. "Hope!" I call. She turns her head in my direction and then cautiously walks towards us. "You remember Matt, right?" I prod.

"Matt," she murmurs, glancing over at him. "I think so, yeah," she agrees, still seeming slightly confused.

"Matt Clark," I elaborate. "His brother Chris sat in front of me all through school," I remind her.

Matt grins at Hope and greets her. "Hi, Hope."

"Hi," she replies. "How's Chris doing?" she inquires.

"He's great. He's in the Navy," he announces.

"No way," I mumble. "Really?"

He nods his head in confirmation. "Yeah, he joined up after college. He's spending Christmas on an aircraft carrier in the South Pacific," he expands.

My eyes widen in surprise. I didn't realize that's what he was doing. "Wow," I mumble. "How are your parents?" I ask.

"Dad's doing better," he reiterates. "Mom is a little stressed," he admits. "How about yours?" he questions.

"They're good! Living in the same house. You know. Nothing much changes in Evergreen Valley," I joke.

"You can say that again," he admits and chuckles softly. He glances at Hope and then back to me in hesitation, before focusing on Hope again. "I'm so sorry about what happened to your mom, Hope," he tells her, sincerely.

Her face instantly falls and my chest tightens watching the pain cross over her face. "Oh. Thanks," she mumbles, automatically.

"How are you doing? I heard you don't leave the ranch," he proclaims, awkwardly.

I cringe as Hope instantly tenses and turns a deep shade of red. I immediately step up to protect her. I force a smile and insist, "Well, you heard wrong." I wrap my arm around her shoulders and pull her into my side. "She's here, right?" I prompt.

Matt gasps and his eyes widen, suddenly realizing his misstep. He nods his head in agreement. "Yeah. Here she is," he broadcasts, solemnly.

"How long have you been back in town?" I ask.

He clears his throat as he turns back to me. "Just a couple of days ago," he enlightens me.

"Well, make sure you tell whoever told you that Hope never leaves the ranch, that she came here to buy a Christmas tree," I emphasize. I have to do something to put an end to the gossip. The last thing she needs is to feel uncomfortable around everyone in town, especially when she made such an effort to leave the ranch. I'm not about to let anything set her back.

"Yeah, sure, okay," he stammers, ineptly.

Hope continues to smile uneasily, obviously not sure what to say. "So, can you help us out?" I request, eager to veer the attention away from Hope.

"Yeah," Matt agrees. "What are you looking for?"

I feel Hope's shoulders instantly relax, grateful for the reprieve. "I need the most perfect tree you have," she announces.

"How big?" he prompts.

I grimace and explain our situation. "We were supposed to get a forty-footer today, but Tommy decided to drop off a four foot tree instead."

Matt laughs and shakes his head in disbelief. "I heard that Tommy was trying to sink the business so he doesn't have to take over, but that's really bad," he reaffirms.

"Tell me about it!" Hope declares, emphatically. "We're hosting the tree lighting this weekend and..."

Matt cuts her off, knowing exactly what she's about to say. "And you don't have a tree," he finishes.

"Exactly," she concurs.

"Got anything to help us out?" I question.

He nods his head slowly in confirmation and mumbles, "I think I can."

"Really?" Hope prods, suddenly buoyant.

"Yeah," he confirms. "It might not be all that big, though. It's so close to Christmas that we're almost picked clean," he reiterates the same thoughts that crossed my mind earlier.

"Yeah, I see that," I acknowledge.

"Alright. Come on," he encourages. "Follow me." Matt strides towards the trees and I let Hope go ahead of me, while I follow behind both of them. After we weave our way through several rows of trees, Matt stops abruptly in front of a thick tree just over four feet tall. Hope's eyes light up, causing my heart to skip a beat. "Alright, this is it," Matt announces. "I know it's not as tall as you want, but," he begins, tentatively.

Hope interrupts him and gleefully declares, "It's perfect."

"Yeah?" he prompts.

"Matt, it's perfect," she claims. "It's the perfect Christmas tree," she reiterates. Then she steps towards Matt and throws her arms around his waist, hugging him tightly. His eyes widen in surprise and he awkwardly pats her on the back. "Thank you," she mumbles into his chest.

She takes a step back and he replies, "You're welcome."

"I know exactly what I'm going to do with it," she states, her excitement obvious. "Thank you!" she repeats.

I smile at Hope, my heart racing at her happiness. I force myself to look at Matt and inquire, "How much?"

He waves me off with a shake of his head and insists, "No charge."

"What?" Hope questions, in shock.

"No charge," he reiterates. "You take it, Hope," he maintains. "Consider it our contribution to the tree lighting. From my family to yours," he offers.

"Matt, thank you so much," she expresses, gratefully. "That's so sweet of you," she proclaims.

I reach out and shake Matt's hand in appreciation. "Really awesome, man. Thanks," I emphasize.

"My pleasure. Truly," he accentuates. "Come on, help me get it in your truck," he offers. Hope jumps up and down in excitement as Matt walks over to grab a saw from the small tractor's trailer. He strides over to the tree and leans down, underneath the branches and begins to saw.

"Thank you," I repeat. He glances up at me and prods, "You want in on this?"

I shrug and nod in agreement, "Sure." He stands up and I lay down under the tree, taking his place. I grasp the handle and keep sawing the trunk of the tree.

"You're a natural," he jokes.

I chuckle and continue sawing until the tree falls to the ground. I grab the tree and carry it over to the trailer, laying it down in the back. Matt slides into the seat of the tractor and drives it up to my truck, while Hope and I take our time, walking together arm in arm. By the time we arrive at my truck, Matt already has the tree strapped down in the back of my pick-up. I reach out to shake his hand and he does the same. "Thanks Matt," I reiterate.

"I'm happy to help," he declares. "We should catch up sometime soon," he suggests.

I grin and agree, "Sounds great. Give me a call when you have some time and I'll do the same."

He nods his head in agreement and waves. "Bye." Then he turns and walks towards another customer. I lean on the side of my truck and look across it at Hope. I smile at her, my heart beating erratically. "What?" she prods, apprehensively.

I shake my head in awe and reply, "Nothing. I was just wondering, if you would like to check out the new restaurant with me while we're out?" I blurt out. I've wanted to take her out for years and now that I have her off the ranch, I'm not going to miss my chance by staying silent.

She grins and replies, "I'd love to," completely shocking me.

I attempt to gulp down the sudden lump in my throat. I don't bother hiding my grin as I happily mumble, "Okay." I walk around the truck and hold out my hand to her, enjoying the small smile playing on her lips. I take a deep breath to calm my own pounding heart. "Should we walk?" I suggest.

"Okay," she easily agrees, slipping her hand into mine. My heart warms even more at her touch, if that's possible. I give her hand a light squeeze, as we stroll towards Mulberry Street Café for lunch, before she has a chance to change her mind.

Chapter 16

Hope

I look out the window on my side of the truck; prepared to keep my eyes open for the ride home. This drive used to be so familiar to me and now it feels as if everything is new again. I watch as town quickly disappears, replaced by rolling hills, brown and green fields, trees, with most of their leaves already covering the ground, as well as dark green pine trees, dirt roads and some animals, mostly cows and a few horses. I feel Gabe's eyes on me, nearly every time he glances in my direction, warming me from the inside out. The edge of our ranch comes into view and I glance at Gabe and smile. "Thank you, Gabe," I begin. "For," I pause, "Well, for today," I finish. I don't really know how to put into words what I'm feeling. I'm just grateful he was there with me the whole way. I wouldn't have wanted it any other way.

He reaches for my hand and gives it a light squeeze, causing my cheeks to instantly warm. "I'm happy I was the one that was by your side today, Hope. Thank you," he proclaims.

Tingles start in my stomach and swiftly burst into the rest of my body at his admission. I take a deep breath and look out the window as we approach the ranch, momentarily overwhelmed with emotion. Gabe releases my hand and honks the horn, twice quickly in succession, as we pull into the circular driveway, the gravel crunching under his tires. He puts his truck in park and turns to me, a proud grin lighting up his face. I return his smile and break his gaze, suddenly feeling fidgety. I unbuckle my seatbelt, while he does the same and then he jumps out of the truck, while I move a little slower climbing out and shut the door behind me.

My sister comes flying out the front door of the inn, followed much slower by Ethan. "Hope!" she screams.

"We got a tree!" I proudly announce, just as my feet hit the ground.

She runs right to me and throws her arms around me, knocking me a little off balance. She wraps me up in a tight hug and I easily return it, as I regain my footing. "I'm so proud of you," she declares, enthusiastically.

I grimace into her shoulder and pretend I don't know what she's talking about. I'm excited, but I don't want everyone to make a huge deal out of this. I pretend that I don't know what she's talking about and prompt, "For getting a tree?"

She releases me and takes a step back, looking at me as if I'm being ridiculous. "No!" she denies. "For leaving the ranch and riding in the truck!" she happily explains.

I feel myself blush and I quickly look away from them, trying to hide my embarrassment. I guess I've just had enough of people feeling sorry for me. I don't want anyone's pity, especially my family and definitely not in front of someone I barely know. "Oh. That. Yeah, well," I stutter, shifting uncomfortably on my toes.

"Ethan, give me a hand with this, will you?" Gabe requests. Gabe knows me so well.

"Yeah, sure," Ethan instantly agrees. He strides towards Gabe, without another glance in my direction.

I quietly breathe a sigh of relief and allow myself to relax. I glance over at Gabe, smiling to myself. I'm thankful he's pulling the attention away from me, as he and Ethan work on untying the tree from the back of the truck. He always seems to know exactly what I need or want even before I utter a word. "You know where to put it, right Gabe?" I question, for clarification.

He grins broadly, causing my stomach to twist into knots. "Yeah," he agrees, with a firm nod of his head. "Go make dinner for the guests," he encourages. He looks me in the eyes and reassures me, "We got this."

"You sure?" I prod.

"Yeah," he verifies with quiet confidence.

"Thanks," I tell him softly and offer him another appreciative smile. I gulp down the lump in my throat and watch him for a moment while he works. I have to admit, I'm truly grateful for him. He's the one person, besides my family, that has always been by my side and I love him for it. My heart clenches tightly at my internal admission, but I know it's true. I just wish I knew what he really thought of me. Joy steps closer to me again and puts her arm around me, pulling me out of my reverie.

She turns me around and leads me towards the inn. "Come on," she encourages, "I'll help," she offers.

My mouth drops open in surprise and I inquire, "What about the horses?"

"They're fed," she informs me. "We can groom them after dinner," she firmly suggests, not leaving room for argument.

"Deal," I agree, as we walk inside together. I slip my coat off and turn towards the front office, while Joy goes right to the kitchen.

I hang my coat on a hook just inside the front office and find my dad. He stands up and walks around the front desk to greet me. He stops in front of me with a big smile on his face, tears in his eyes and opens his arms wide. I step into his arms without a word and wrap my arms around his waist as he envelops me in a warm, protective hug. "I know you don't want me to make a big deal out of this, but I just need to say this. I'm so incredibly proud of you, Hope," he whispers, emphatically into the top of my head.

I feel his warm breath in my hair and I squeeze him a little tighter. My emotions begin to claw their way from my chest and up my throat, bringing tears to my eyes. I attempt to blink them back, fighting them and refusing to let them fall right now. "I'm sorry," I murmur.

He immediately interrupts, "Don't apologize, Sweetheart. Don't ever apologize for this," he insists, his voice catching. "You needed to do things in your own time. I've just been worried about you," he adds, as he rubs comforting circles down my back.

I sigh heavily, feeling content, as I lean into his chest. "I love you, Daddy," I mumble, my voice a hoarse whisper.

"I love you, too, Hope," he rasps. "Your mom would be proud of you too," he adds, still sounding choked up.

"Thanks, Dad," I murmur.

He kisses the top of my head and gives me another squeeze. I take a deep breath and exhale slowly as I wiggle out of his embrace and he reluctantly releases me. I take a step back and clear my throat. Then I inform him, "I'm going to go work on dinner for the guests. Joy offered to help and she's already in the kitchen."

He chuckles softly and prompts, "You better go join her, then."

I smile at him and turn around, quickly making my way towards the kitchen to join my sister. I immediately walk over to the sink and wash my hands, while Joy begins pulling ingredients out of the refrigerator. I dry my hands on the dishtowel by the sink and spin around. I turn on the stove as Joy boosts herself up onto the countertop and begins eating a carrot, making me giggle. Both dad and I have found that Joy's way of helping in the kitchen, always seems to be her sitting somewhere in the room and snacking, while she watches me doing the actual cooking. Thankfully, she does usually help with the cleanup.

"I can't believe you left," Joy mumbles, with clear awe.

"Neither can I," I finally admit, a satisfied smile on my lips. It may be hard for even me to believe I left, but I'm really glad I decided to go with him today. Plus, I ended up having a wonderful time with Gabe.

She tilts her head to the side and narrows her eyes, assessing me, as if she can read my mind. "Why did you?" she finally blurts out.

"We needed a tree for the tree lighting," I declare, stating the obvious.

She gives me a doubtful look and arches her eyebrows in challenge. "Gabe could have gotten the tree, Hope," she reminds me.

I heave a sigh, knowing she's right. In fact, Gabe offered to do exactly that, but I didn't want him to go without me. I felt like I needed to be with him, but that sounds silly. "I don't know," I concede, shrugging my shoulders. "I really don't. I just really wanted to go," I emphasize.

"Well, I'm glad you did," she claims, with a raw honesty. My heart catches in my throat, as I realize how much I've affected Joy and dad with the way I've been dealing with everything since the accident. I guess I've always known it, but right now I see it in her eyes. I gulp down the lump in my throat as I reach for the chicken, trying to ignore the small sense of unease in my belly.

"So am I," I confess. My thoughts drift back to earlier today, walking hand in hand alongside Gabe to go out for lunch. "Gabe and I even went to Mulberry Street Café for lunch," I inform her. I glance in her direction to see her reaction, my own smile on display as thoughts of our date run through my mind. I suddenly pause, wondering if it was a date to him. I shake my head and immediately push the thought out of my head, as I turn back to the stove. I can't think about it right now.

"Really?" she challenges, wide-eyed.

"Yes," I confirm, with a nod. "It was nice," I murmur, attempting to downplay how much fun I had with him this afternoon. "We walked over there from Matt's Tree Farm and then back," I reveal.

"How did it feel?" she prods, curiously. I grimace at her question and shrug, thinking about the one thing that was really hard to ignore. "What's the matter?" she prompts.

I heave a heavy sigh, before I stop what I'm doing and turn towards her, fully meeting her gaze. "I just wish people wouldn't make such a big deal over it," I concede.

She winces and immediately apologizes. "I'm sorry. I've just been so worried about you," she explains. She jumps off the counter and walks over to my left to the pumpkin pie. She cuts herself a small slice and puts it on a dessert plate. Then she reaches for a fork and leans over the counter, ready to dig in.

"I know," I acknowledge, but that's not what's bothering me. "I know people have been talking about me," I convey, thinking back to what Matt disclosed without thinking.

She takes a bite of her pie, considering me. "I don't know about that," she mumbles and takes another bite of pie.

"No, they have," I insist. "Matt even said something at the tree farm and Mrs. Hensen," I pause and shake my head in irritation before I continue, "she looked like she saw a ghost," I complain.

She scrunches her nose up with distaste. "Was it really that bad?" she prompts, her voice full of concern.

I nod in confirmation, "Yeah, but Gabe was great," I praise. "He was just really," I pause, trying to think of how to describe it, "I don't know," I mutter and then I finally decide on, "protective."

"He loves you, Hope," she states, matter of fact.

I gasp and my heart skips a beat, wishing her words were the truth. I shake my head in denial and plead, "Stop."

"I'm serious," she claims, emphatically. "He really cares about you," she declares. She looks into my eyes as if a look alone can convince me it's the truth.

My heartbeat quickens and I bite my lower lip, wondering if it could really be true. Sometimes I think we could be together, but I've been dealing with so much for so long and I didn't want him to feel like he had to be there for me. I didn't want to hold him back and besides, he only ever treats me as a friend or even as a sister. I grimace, irritated at the thought of Gabe treating me like a sister. That's not what I want. Have I just been looking at it wrong? I glance at Joy and she seems to genuinely believe what she's saying. "Do you really think so?" I prod, wishing it were true.

"He loves you, as much as you love him," she apprises me, with complete confidence.

"Joy!" I yell her name, scolding her for verbalizing what I feel for him in my heart, without my consent. I stare at her with wide eyes, as my whole body instantly turns red.

She smirks, mischievously and pushes me a little more. "Deny it," she challenges, arching her eyebrows. I begin mashing the potatoes, trying to hide my smile, quietly admitting my truth. Joy throws her head back and laughs. Then she looks at me as if she just won an award and chants, "That's all I needed to know."

I laugh as she takes another bite of her pumpkin pie, complete satisfaction written all over her face. Then I turn back towards the stove, a hesitant smile on my lips as I continue working on dinner for everyone. If what she says is true, maybe it's time to find out.

Chapter 17

Ethan

I push another hay bale in place to help support the Christmas tree Gabe picked out with Hope today. Gabe and I raised it up on hay bales to make it appear bigger than it actually is. We strung colored lights around the tree before we raised it, to make it a little easier to do. "Let's string more lights along the hay bales underneath the tree," Gabe suggests. "That should help it appear a little bigger too," he murmurs. I walk over to the box, and grab another string of colored lights. I make sure it's all untangled before I begin to wrap the lights around the hay, while Gabe sets up the extension cords to hook all the lights together. Then, we spread loose hay over all the wires to make it appear more natural. Gabe pauses and takes a step back, assessing our work. "I think this is how she wanted it," he mumbles.

"I hope so," I grumble. "Hauling those hay bales was no joke," I declare.

Gabe smirks as he looks over at me. "You need to toughen up, city boy," he jokes. Although, we both know his comment does hold some weight.

I huff a laugh and mutter, "Right."

"Take this," Gabe instructs, as he hands me a large rake. Then he moves to pick up another hay bale, putting it in place for seating around the Christmas tree. He sets it down, then he inquires, "How's the book coming?"

"You know, it's actually coming along pretty well," I admit. A small smile lights up my face, as an image of Joy crosses my mind. It seems she has been a wonderful inspiration for me.

"Yeah?" Gabe prompts, with an arch of his eyebrows. He walks over to the wheelbarrow and grabs a little more hay, spreading it out over the cords.

"Yeah," I nod in confirmation. "I hate to admit that Amanda was right, but..." I trail off with a shrug of my shoulders.

Gabe stops and looks me in the eyes. "Do yourself a favor and tell her she was right," he suggests. "It will go a long way," he insists. Then he reclaims the rake from me and continues smoothing out the hay scattered all over the ground.

My cell phone rings in my coat pocket. I pull it out and glance at the screen, Amanda's face lighting it up. "Oh, speak of the devil," I mumble, holding my phone up in indication. "Excuse me, would you?" I request, glancing at Gabe.

"Sure," he acknowledges and goes right back to work.

I saunter towards the stables to answer Amanda's phone call, while Gabe continues readjusting the hay around the tree, attempting to get it perfect. I stop right next to the corner of the stables as I tap my phone to answer. "Hi, Amanda," I greet her.

"Ethan, darling!" she exclaims. "How is life on the ranch?" she inquires. Although, we're both aware of what she really wants to know, she always remains polite.

I take a deep breath before I open my mouth to speak. "I don't often admit when I'm wrong, but I will certainly admit that you were right," I concede, graciously.

"Oh?" she questions, obviously intrigued.

I chuckle softly at her reaction. "I was blocked," I finally admit, nodding my head, even though she can't see me. "I needed this trip. You were right," I proclaim.

I hear the smile in her voice as she happily replies, "I knew it. Does that mean I'll have my Valentine's Day book?" she prods.

"I've only been here a couple of days, Amanda," I remind her. I'm not quite sure if that's a promise I want to make when I still have so much work left to do.

"But..." she urges, dragging out the word.

I wince, but I know I can do it if I focus. I know exactly where I want to go with this story. I just need the time to get all the details down and I will have that here. "But, yes," I happily confirm. "I do have an idea. I even wrote an outline last night," I inform her, hoping to appease her.

"Really?" she prompts, her excitement palpable. "That's excellent news! I'm so glad to hear it," she announces.

"I know I'll have my first draft by the time I leave here," I update her, with even more confidence than I started this conversation with.

"I can't wait," she proclaims. "Ciao, Ethan," she states.

"Bye," I reply. Then I disconnect the call, just as Mr. Deeds, a beautiful, black, Tennessee Walking horse, sticks his head out of the stable and nudges me, gently with his nose. I chuckle and pet the side of his head and neck. He always seems to be looking for attention. "What are you looking at?" I ask Mr. Deeds, smirking. I slip my phone back in my coat pocket and give the horse another gentle pat, before I turn away. I stride back to the corral towards Gabe, ready to help him finish up with the tree.

Gabe stands as I approach him, wiping his hands on his jeans to get the hay off. "All good?" he questions, with an arch of his eyebrow.

"All good," I confirm, nodding my head. "Took your advice and she's as happy as a clam," I inform him.

"Told you," Gabe says, grinning.

"Is that what you do with Hope?" I probe.

He shrugs and admits, "Sometimes. Joy, too. Depends on their mood. It's about smoothing things over before there can be a fight," he explains.

I nod in understanding. "It's good advice," I compliment.

The corners of his mouth twitch up in amusement. "Yeah, well," he begins. "I don't give it very often."

Gabe grasps the handles of the wheelbarrow and lifts, striding for the stables. I follow him and briefly hesitate, before I tell myself just to ask. I blurt out, "So what's Joy's story?"

He pauses and looks at me with a quirk of his eyebrows. "What do you mean?" he prods.

"She told me all about Hope, but never mentioned anything about herself," I explain. "Well, except for going off to college," I add.

He nods in acknowledgment and then continues sauntering slowly towards the stables, pushing the wheelbarrow in front of him. "Yeah, she went away, while Hope stayed close. She was always more of a homebody," he elaborates.

"Joy isn't?" I prompt.

He shakes his head and attempts to explain, "No. Not since their mom passed. Joy came home from college, but she's got itchy feet."

"Itchy feet?" I repeat, needing clarification.

"She wants to travel. She leaves the ranch any chance she can get. She always talks about how she wants to see the world and all these places she wants to travel to," he elaborates.

"Really?" I question, smiling to myself. It seems we have more in common than she's letting me know. I just wish she would share more of this with me herself.

"Yeah," he confirms. "She did a semester abroad in Italy," he adds.

"No kidding," I mumble, reverently, grinning wider. "I did too," I inform him.

He gives me a crooked smile. "Well, that's something else you've got in common," he acknowledges.

My eyebrows draw down in confusion. "Something else?" I prompt. "What's the first thing?" I ask, curiously.

His eyes widen, seeming surprised I don't already know what he's referring to. "She's a writer," he clarifies.

I gasp, as my eyes widen in shock. I freeze momentarily, as Gabe continues to stride for the barn. I quickly pull myself out of my daze and jog to catch up with him. "You can't drop a bomb like that and just walk away," I insist.

He chuckles and prods, "A bomb?"

"I literally know nothing about this woman and you just tell me that she's a writer," I broadcast, slightly stunned. "What kind of writer? Did she go to school for it?" I ramble, wanting to know everything.

He chuckles and urges, "Slow down." He begins loading more hay into the wheelbarrow with a pitchfork, while he talks. "She got her degree in journalism," he tells me. He pauses and gives a shake of his head in disbelief. "You really need to talk to her more. She's a tough one to get to open up," he concedes.

I grimace and grumble, "So I've noticed."

"She's always been like that. No one really knows what she's thinking, except maybe Hope," he informs me.

"How far apart in age are they?" I ask.

"Three and a half years," he enlightens me.

"She have a boyfriend or anything?" I inquire. My hands start sweating as my nerves increase, making me feel like a teenage boy again.

He huffs a laugh and his eyes widen. "Joy?" he prompts, making sure he heard me right. I nod in acknowledgement, holding my breath, as I await his response. "No," he finally replies. "Not that I know of. Not unless she's hiding him from us," he continues.

I can't stop the sigh of relief that slips from my lips. "Good," I mumble, a smile tugging at the corners of my mouth.

"Good?" he questions, arching his eyebrows in challenge.

My eyes widen and I feel my face heat instantly. I stammer, "Um, I...I mean..."

He chuckles and then grins broadly in amusement. "Yeah, I know what you mean," he confirms with a nod of his head. He sets the pitchfork down, leaning it against the barn wall.

I give myself a mental shake and take a deep breath. Then I attempt to turn the focus away from me, "How long have you and Hope been together?" I inquire, curiously.

Gabe bursts out laughing as he picks up the wheelbarrow and pushes it out of the barn. I quickly follow him, puzzled by his reaction. He stops at Toby's horse stable and feeds him, filling his trough with hay. Toby is a beautiful dark brown thoroughbred. I watch him, waiting for him to explain. My eyebrows draw down in bewilderment and I prompt, "What did I say?"

A strange look comes over his face, but he quickly masks it before I'm able to decipher his look. "Hope and I aren't together," he declares.

"What are you talking about?" I question. "Did you break up?" I prompt, instantly feeling bad for bringing it up.

He grimaces and shakes his head in denial. "We've never been together," he insists.

My mouth drops open in shock and I can't help but ask, "Ever?" I give my head a slight shake trying to make sense of what he's saying. "Not even in high school?" I elaborate.

He sighs heavily and makes his way to the next stable to feed Sport, while he begins to explain. "No, I'm a year older than she is. We've known each other literally our entire lives," he emphasizes. He pauses, as a look of pure sadness passes through his eyes. "She looks at me like a brother," he mutters, grumpily.

I chuckle and shake my head, denying his statement. "No, she doesn't," I declare, with absolutely no doubt in my mind I'm right.

"What are you talking about? Of course she does," he states.

I arch my eyebrows in challenge. "Gabe, if any sister looked at a brother like that, I'd be a little concerned," I joke.

He shakes his head, refusing to believe me. "You have no idea what you're talking about," he reiterates.

I smirk and claim, "You're just in denial."

"No, I'm not," he insists, still shaking his head.

"Joy is the one that said she looks at you like a brother," I remind him. "Not Hope," I emphasize.

He stops and turns to stare at me and I see a sudden change in his eyes as he processes my words. He exhales slowly and admits, "I have been in love with that girl my entire life."

I grin broadly and with a touch of pride I announce, "I knew it."

"We even went to prom together," he enlightens me. "As friends, of course," he adds, as an afterthought.

I smirk and sarcastically mumble, "Oh, of course."

"Do you think I work on the ranch because I love horses?" he challenges.

"No," I answer, assuming what his response will be.

"No!" he declares, vehemently. "When Hope's mom died, Hope spiraled downward. Frank was so badly injured and Joy was dealing with it on her own. I came here to be with Hope. To help her," he proclaims.

"To protect her?" I prod.

He nods in agreement. "Yeah. And you know what?" he prompts, not really wanting me to answer. "Today was the first time in nearly five years that she stepped foot off this ranch," he states, his pride for her obvious.

"I heard," I tell him.

"And she got in a car," he adds.

"I saw," I acknowledge.

"And she went to lunch," he informs me.

"Really?" I ask, surprised after everything I've heard.

He nods in confirmation and exclaims, "Yes! In public!" He pauses and shakes his head, as if struggling to believe reality himself, before he continues. "I feel like if I wasn't close by," he stops and gulps, his Adam's apple bobbing up and down. Then he restarts, trying again to tell me what he was thinking. "If I wasn't around, I would never see her and I would lose her," he concludes, sorrowfully.

"So, now what?" I prod.

"I...I don't know," he stammers.

"Does she know how you feel?" I probe, intrigued.

He huffs a laugh and prompts, "How could she not?"

I smirk and challenge, "Well, you didn't see how she looks at you. Maybe she doesn't know how you feel about her."

I watch him, as he momentarily gets lost in his thoughts. Then he murmurs, almost inaudibly, "Maybe." He takes a deep breath and exhales slowly as he looks over at me. "So, you have any advice for me?" he solicits.

I laugh at the thought of giving relationship advice with my history. "I'm hardly the person that you should ask for romantic advice," I mumble, honestly.

"Yeah, why's that?" he questions, as we reach the stable to feed Mr. Deeds. He fills his trough, then he turns around and heads back to the barn, while I trudge slowly behind.

When I step into the barn, Gabe is already putting the wheelbarrow back where he got it. I sigh and start to tell him my story, as simply as possible in explanation. "A year and a half ago, I proposed to my college sweetheart," I inform him, with a grimace.

"Really?" Gabe probes, wide eyed.

I take a deep breath in and exhale slowly, trying not to really think about it. "Yes," I confirm. "I took her to the top of the Empire State Building, just like the end of her favorite movie."

"And?" he urges.

"I got down on one knee, held out the ring and proposed," I confess.

"What happened?" he questions.

I purse my lips and then I quickly blurt out, "She started crying and told me that she was in love with someone else."

He flinches noticeably and mumbles, "Ouch. That hurts."

I nod my head in agreement and grumble, "You have no idea."

"What did you do?" he prompts.

"I left," I reply. I shrug my shoulders, attempting to brush it off, but that kind of rejection is hard to forget.

"You left..." he trails off waiting for more. When I don't continue he finishes with a question, "town?"

I shake my head and sigh heavily. "No, I left. I stood up, got in the elevator and left her crying on the observation deck. I haven't seen her since," I concede.

"Wow," Gabe murmurs, sympathetically.

I nod my head in acknowledgement. "Unfortunately, I haven't been able to write one single word since then either," I elaborate.

"Well, until you got here," Gabe reminds me.

I nod my head and the corners of my lips curve up in satisfaction. "Yeah," I mumble, as bright blue eyes cross my mind. "As soon as I met Joy, actually," I add, thoughtfully.

"Really?" he prompts, with a small smile.

"Yeah," I confirm, "and now I have an idea for a book that I know my publisher is going to love," I reveal.

"That's great," he declares and pauses, "but it really doesn't help me much though," he adds.

I laugh at his assessment of my story. "I never said it would." Then I pause, momentarily; as I think about everything he's been through with Hope. "Listen, Gabe, I don't know you or Hope, but I can see the connection you have. I'm sure everyone can," I claim. "You need to think of where you see yourself in five, ten, even twenty years from now and ask yourself if you see Hope with you," I advise.

Gabe nods in acknowledgement, obviously deep in thought. "I need to get some writing done," I apprise him, knowing he probably needs time to himself to think.

"Yeah," he mumbles. "Goodnight."

"Goodnight," I proclaim, as I walk out of the barn. I quickly stride for my room, excited to get on my laptop and get to work. I want to get my ideas down now, while they're overflowing and fresh in my mind.

Chapter 18

Gabe

I watch as Ethan walks away, wondering if he could be right? Does Hope really have feelings for me? I heave a sigh, knowing I would give almost anything for that to be true. I just need to talk to her and tell her how I feel. My stomach twists with anxiety at just the thought of finally telling her what I've been feeling for so long. What will she think? I try to gulp down the lump in my throat. Ethan's right though, I have to tell her. I can't keep living like this, hoping we might have a chance one day.

After the accident everything changed. I didn't think I had a right to tell her how I felt, when she was dealing with so much and just trying to make it through every day unscathed. She needed to come first. But things have changed again, for both of us. I need our one-day to be one day soon, or I'm going to have to make some difficult choices with my life. Choices that could change everything I know. I don't know if I'm ready for that, especially when some ends are definitely something I don't want. My biggest problem with that kind of change, I can't imagine my life without Hope. I don't want to. She's everything to me.

I take a deep breath and exhale slowly to calm my anxiety, just as the familiar black barn cat scrambles underneath the feed table. He looks up at me as if judging me. I huff a humorless laugh and mutter, "What are you looking at?" He tilts his head to the side, as if urging me on. I heave a sigh and murmur, "I know, I know." I can't wait anymore. I guess it's time for me to find out what Hope is really thinking and if she could ever picture us as a couple. I need to know if we have a chance for a future and there's really only one way to find out.

I stride out of the barn, intent on finding Hope and talking to her. I look up and smile, immediately spotting her. My steps slow as I stare at her, sitting outside on the back stoop. She's staring at the Christmas tree in admiration. My heart skips a beat at the sight of her. She looks absolutely beautiful, deep in thought with a small smile on her face. I slowly approach her, enjoying the moments before she realizes I'm there. I swiftly close the distance, the instant she knows I'm there. I give a nod in the direction of the tree and prompt, "So what do you think?"

She grins up at me, her whole face lighting up with her happiness. My own smile widens as I look down at her, taking in her reaction. I lower myself onto the stoop, sitting down right next to her. I prop my elbows on my knees and let my hands hang loosely between my legs, feeling the warmth of her body next to mine. "It's perfect," she praises, with awe in her voice. "It's exactly how I envisioned it," she happily declares.

I silently breathe a sigh of relief, pleased with her reaction. "Yup, it's all ready for the guests to come tomorrow and decorate," I gladly inform her.

She offers me an appreciative smile. "You worked really hard on this, Gabe," she acknowledges. Her simple gesture warms me from the inside out. Doesn't she realize I would do anything for her? "Thank you," she states, gratefully.

"Ethan helped, too," I add.

She turns to me and arches her eyebrows in challenge, causing me to chuckle. "I'm sure you did most of it," she proclaims.

"Yeah, well," I stammer, rubbing the back of my neck, awkwardly. I'm thankful it's dark out here, so she can't see my face turning such a deep shade of red, all because of her confidence in me. "He is from the city," I mumble under my breath, as if that's enough of an explanation.

She laughs and the lighthearted sound sends chills down my spine. "Thank you, Gabe," she reiterates. "You're too good to me," she declares.

I shake my head in denial. Nothing would ever be too good for her. "No, I'm not," I insist. I can always do more when it comes to Hope and she should know that by now. Maybe Ethan's right. Maybe she doesn't know how I feel.

She turns her head and looks at me. Her soft brown eyes hold my gaze, appearing determined. "But you are," she maintains, emphatically.

"Come on, Hope. I'd do anything for you," I finally confess. She needs to know the truth in my statement. "Don't you know that?" I practically plead with her to see the truth in my eyes. I stare at her, assessing her reaction and hoping it's finally time for us.

She cautiously reaches up towards me and lovingly runs her thumb along my cheek. My skin tingles from her touch and my stomach twists with hope. My heart immediately begins to race as I look into her eyes, suddenly the color of melted chocolate. Kissing her is the only thing I want right now. This moment finally feels right and I'm not about to waste another minute. I slowly lean in towards her, glancing from her eyes to her lips, letting her know my intention, before I return my gaze to her eyes. She tilts her head perfectly towards me in anticipation, causing a quick intake of breath. My heart pounds so hard, I feel as if it will burst right out of my chest. She's so close that I can feel her sweet, warm breath mixing with mine. I gulp down the lump in my throat as I start to close the final distance between us.

The sliding glass door behind us flies open, instantly startling us apart. "This looks amazing!" Joy croons. My heart instantly sinks at our missed chance. I feel Joy's steely gaze focused on both Hope and me, while both of us remain silent and I try to catch my breath. "Oh, no," she grumbles. "I'm sorry," she apologizes. "Did I interrupt something?" she probes.

"No, not at all," Hope instantly replies, with a quick shake of her head. My whole body tenses at her response, while my heart sinks into the pit of my stomach. Does she really mean that? Or does she just not want Joy to know? I gulp hard, not liking either option.

"Are you sure?" Joy prompts, hesitantly.

I stare at Hope for a minute, hoping, waiting, to see if she'll change her mind. She just continues to stare out at the Christmas tree, causing my whole body to sag in defeat. "Yeah," I finally grumble my crushed reply.

Joy glances between Hope and me one more time, before she concedes and sits down on my other side. "Gabe, where were you?" she questions.

"In the barn," I answer.

"For an hour?" she challenges.

"Yeah," I confirm. "I got caught up," I reply and heave a sigh. She doesn't need to know I wasn't in there doing something for the horses or the ranch for that matter. And she doesn't need to know I was in there thinking about her sister, especially now that it appears that Hope doesn't feel the same way about me. I take a deep breath to calm my anxiety. I glance at Hope out of the corner of my eye. I know for me, it's always about Hope and I honestly have no idea what to do about it now.

"Caught up doing what?" she pushes. "There's nothing in there," she emphasizes, as if she's telling me something I didn't know.

I pinch my lips tightly together, not knowing how to answer her, especially now that Hope's acting like our almost kiss was a mistake. Is that what she thinks? Does she regret it almost happening? "Just...thinking, okay?" I blurt out, trying to push my negative thoughts out of my head. "I have a lot on my mind," I mumble, irritably.

"Like what?" she prods, innocently.

"Joy! Leave him alone!" Hope scolds her, defending me. My stomach flips, her actions showing she does care, but that almost makes it hurt even worse. "What is this, twenty questions?" she demands.

"Sorry," she apologizes, sarcastically, dragging out the word. "I was just asking," she adds, defensively.

"It's fine," I mumble, dismissively. I give her a wave of my hand, hoping she'll drop it. "There's just a lot to do this week before the tree lighting," I claim, knowing my excuse is feeble.

Hope huffs a laugh and exclaims, "You're telling me! I have to start baking tomorrow, after I get the horses ready for the day," she informs us.

"I have six trail rides with new guests every hour, starting at ten," Joy enlightens us.

"I know," Hope acknowledges. "I'll pack you a lunch," she offers.

Joy looks at Hope and gratefully accepts, "Thanks."

"Just give me a list and I'll get it all done," I instruct, wanting to keep myself busy. At least then I don't have as much time to dwell on my insecurities when it comes to Hope.

"Maybe Ethan wants to pitch in," Joy suggests.

"Ethan?" Hope questions. "He's a guest!" she reiterates.

Joy nods in affirmation. "Yeah, but he wants to learn about ranch life for his book. I told him he could follow us around," she apprises us.

"He's all yours, Gabe," Hope immediately announces. She offers me up as a sacrifice, with barely a glance in my direction.

"Mine? Why?" I challenge.

"Because I hardly think he's gonna' want to watch me bake cookies all day," she reminds me. I wince, knowing she's right.

"And he can't come on the trail rides with me," Joy proclaims. "He hardly knows how to ride," she adds.

I heave a heavy sigh in defeat and grumble, "Great. Exactly what I wanted." I don't mind his help or his company, but I don't think I'm going to be very good at trying to teach anyone anything with my mind so preoccupied.

"He really should know what it's like to be on a horse, considering he's writing a book set on a ranch," Joy mumbles, with a smirk.

"Fine," I grumble my agreement. "I'll take him if I have time," I tell them both. I can figure the rest out tomorrow.

"Thank you," Joy murmurs, gratefully.

"All right. I'm turning in," Hope announces, bringing me down to reality. She puts her hands on her knees and pushes herself up, taking her warmth along with her. I'm immediately disappointed to lose her company, but I bite my lower lip and force myself not to show it. I was hoping we'd still have some time to talk without Joy to clarify what just happened. But, I can't make her stay if all she wants to do is walk away from me, no matter how much I want her to.

"Yeah, me too," Joy agrees. She stands up, following Hope's lead.

I glance up at both of them and mutter, "See you in the morning."

"Night, Gabe," Joy states.

"Goodnight," Hope murmurs.

I look into Hope's big brown eyes, attempting to convey how I'm feeling and what's on my mind. I finally mumble my reply, "Night."

I watch feeling lost, as Joy and Hope disappear into the house together. Hope meets my gaze through the glass after she shuts the door and offers me a small smile, warming my heart again. I return her smile, feeling a small spark of hope, yet again. She hesitates for a moment before she turns away from the door and disappears further inside the house. I exhale harshly and plant the palms of my hands on my knees, pushing myself up off the stoop. Momentarily, I stand in front of the sliding glass door, willing her to reappear. The overhead lights click off in the kitchen and I drop my head, my disappointment overwhelming. I stuff my hands inside my jeans pockets and I reluctantly turn towards the driveway, slowly I trudge all the way to my truck.

I run over the last hour in my head, over and over again. I can't help, but wonder if Hope and I finally would've kissed if Joy hadn't interrupted us. Was she just embarrassed and not ready to say anything to Joy about it yet? Or was she grateful for the interruption? Does she think kissing me would've been a mistake? I grimace and shake my head, refusing to believe that could be true. She looked like she wanted to kiss me, just as much as I wanted to kiss her. I saw her love for me in her eyes. I know I did. Maybe I'm just fooling myself, but maybe that's what I need right now, some kind of sign. I move to pull my hands out of my pockets to open the door of my

155

truck and my fingers brush against cool metal. I pause for a minute, before I pull my hands out of my pockets. I take a deep breath and attempt to stay positive. I can't keep guessing, not until I know for sure. I smile to myself, choosing to believe we have a chance for a future together. For the first time in a very long time, I'm hopeful again. I just need more time with her, just the two of us, without distractions.

Chapter 19

Hope

I reach up and give Cupcake some love, running my hand along his neck, soft, but firm, knowing he loves it. Cupcake is a Paint Thoroughbred horse with unique brown and white markings and he's incredibly sweet. I spin around and grab the saddle I need off the rack and turn back to him, placing it over Cupcake's back. Then I reach down to work on all of the straps, tightening the cinch and adjusting the stirrups. I continue working mindlessly, like I have all morning, with all my thoughts still focused on Gabe.

My stomach flips thinking about how we almost kissed last night. He has a way of making me feel like I'm the only person in his world, like I'm the only thing that matters to him. He's always been there for me, just like I want to be there for him. A soft smile covers my lips and I can't help, but wonder if he is my future. I sure can't imagine my life without him being a part of it.

"Good morning, Hope," Ethan greets me. He strolls into the barn, pulling me from my thoughts. I startle slightly and look up as he approaches me. I instantly notice his clothes. He looks like he's dressed to be on the ranch today. Like me, he's wearing blue jeans and dark brown boots. Although, my jeans are light and my boots are cowboy boots, like usual. He has an olive green fitted t-shirt on, under a flannel colored navy blue and white, with accents of dark green and yellow, topped with a casual brown winter coat. While I'm in a pale, teal green sweater and my navy blue winter coat with a fur accent on the hood.

"Ethan, Hi," I reply, offering him a welcoming smile. "You're up early," I comment.

He nods his head in acknowledgement and flashes me a grin. "Joy told me that you'd let me help you if I got here early enough," he informs me.

I wince at the hopeful look on his face. "I just finished," I announce.

His eyes widen in surprise and he prompts, "All of the horses?"

I give him a look of apology, remembering what Joy had said about him wanting to help us out and learn more about the ranch. "Yeah, I started at six," I apprise him. "I've got a lot to do today," I add.

"Is there anything I can do to help?" he offers.

I shake my head, regretful. "No, but thanks," I tell him appreciatively.

He heaves a sigh of disappointment and grumbles, "Oh."

I can't help but feel bad for him. I unhitch Cupcake from the tethers and glance in his direction. "I have a little time, Ethan. Would you like to go for a ride?" I suggest.

He shifts nervously on his feet. "Oh, I don't ride," he denounces. "I don't know how," he explains. "I've never been on a horse."

I smile at him, in attempt to help him feel more comfortable. "We can just go in the corral. I'll hold him," I propose.

"Like a pony ride?" he questions, appearing confused.

I can't stop the laugh that bursts out of my chest. "Yeah, I guess," I concede. "I'll teach you how to mount and dismount," I elaborate.

He pauses momentarily as he thinks about my offer. Then he tilts his head to the side and looks down at me with the corners of his mouth curving upwards. "Can we call it something besides a pony ride?" he inquires.

I laugh again and remind him, "Those were your words, not mine!"

He nods in admission and mumbles, "True."

"What about calling it research for your book?" I suggest.

Ethan smiles appreciatively. "Much better," he concurs.

"Come on. He's ready," I tell him.

A nervous look crosses his face again and I grab a black riding helmet for him on our way out of the stable. We step into the smaller corral and I hand him the helmet. "Here," I murmur, as I hand him the helmet. "Put this on," I instruct.

He takes it from me and places it on his head. Then he hooks the strap underneath his chin and looks at me, anxiously. "Okay," he agrees.

I help Ethan climb up into the saddle, by placing his foot in the stirrup and easily pulling himself over. I show him how to hold the reigns and instruct him on how to use them, before I begin leading Cupcake around the ring. I glance up at Ethan and grin at the wide, proud smile lighting up his face, as he quickly becomes comfortable. As we begin our third lap around the ring, he questions, "Is this considered trotting?"

I bite the inside of my cheek, holding back my laugh. I love seeing the happiness and enjoyment on his face and I know I would only ruin it by laughing. "No," I reply. "You're not ready for trotting yet. This is just walking," I enlighten him.

"I can see why you love horses so much," he admits.

"I love everything about them," I mumble, honestly.

"I haven't seen you ride," he comments, observantly.

I hide my grimace and focus on guiding Cupcake around the ring. "I don't ride anymore," I finally concede.

His eyebrows draw down in confusion. "Bad experience?" he probes.

I heave a sigh and vaguely mumble, "Something like that." My mind begins to wander to the last time I rode and I reflexively cringe. I clear my throat and glance at him. "Are you ready to get off yet," I prod.

He nods in agreement. "Yeah, I know you've got a lot on your plate," he claims.

"Maybe Gabe or Joy can give you another lesson," I suggest. I feel bad for cutting his lesson short, even though it was an impromptu one, but I need some time alone to pull myself together.

"That would be great," he agrees.

"Do you want me to get the mounting block for you?" I ask.

He shakes his head and insists, "No, I should be fine. I got on without it. I'm sure I can get off," he replies, with mock confidence.

I arch my eyebrows in challenge and relent, "Okay. Be careful," I insist. I take a small step back, maintaining my hold on Cupcake's lead. "It's not like the movies," I tell him. "If you just want to take your foot out of the stirrup and slide down," I suggest. "Watch out when you land. The mud is slippery, especially when it's cold," I inform him.

"Like this?" he prompts. He swings his left leg over Cupcake and slides down his side, landing on both feet.

I smile at his successful dismount. "Great job!" I praise.

He grins, full of pride. Then he offers, "Can I help you bring him back to his stall?"

"No, Eddie is coming to get him," I tell him.

"Eddie?" he questions.

"He's another ranch hand," I explain, just as Eddie steps up to us. He's a tall thin man, with dark brown hair, soft brown eyes and currently has a 5 o'clock shadow. He's always been a little quiet, but he's great with the animals. He's wearing dark blue jeans with a light blue and dark blue-checkered flannel along with a tan and white shearling coat and work boots.

"You guys talking about me?" he questions, as he approaches. He pulls his black knit, winter hat down over his ears.

"Eddie Morris," I declare, "Meet Ethan Dulane."

Ethan reaches out and smiles as he shakes his hand. "Pleasure," he states.

"Hey," Eddie replies, with an absent-minded nod of his head. "Is Cupcake ready?" he inquires.

"He's all yours," I reply.

Eddie takes the reigns from me and quietly responds, "Thanks." Then he turns and leads Cupcake away and back behind the stables, towards a trail leading over to the indoor riding ring.

Ethan arches his eyebrows and mumbles, "Charming guy."

The corners of my mouth twitch up in amusement. Ethan turns back towards me and my eyes widen as he takes a step towards a deep mud puddle. I quickly lunge forward to stop him. "Watch out!" I exclaim. He startles at my outburst and slips. I reach out to grab him to keep him from falling. He grasps onto me, instinctively spinning, trying to protect me, as we both stumble towards the ground. He tumbles backwards, landing hard as I fall on top of him. I gasp in shock and plant my hands on the ground on either side of him for leverage, while he still tightly grasps my sides, a little stunned. I look down at him, our eyes wide and our noses barely an inch apart. "Are you okay?" I ask, as I attempt to shake off my own surprise.

"What's going on here?" Gabe calls out, his pain obvious.

My head snaps up to find Gabe, standing stiffly wearing his familiar jeans and tan work boots with a black t-shirt, covered with a red and black-checkered flannel and his brown corduroy and wool work coat. His stormy green eyes are glaring down at both Ethan and me, making me flinch. My heart skips a beat at the look of betrayal on his face.

"Oh, hey, Gabe," Ethan mumbles, getting his voice back.

"Hey, yourself," Gabe snaps. He shakes his head looking devastated, as he spins on his heel and stalks off towards the barn.

My heart pounds rapidly as panic starts to build inside me as the reality of what just happened hits me like a pile of bricks. I push off the ground and jump up quickly, before I take off, running after him. "Gabe!" I yell, desperately. "Gabe, wait," I repeat. I follow him out through the fence and out of the corral.

He storms into the barn, knowing I'm right behind, chasing after him. He grabs the wheelbarrow and moves it towards the stacks of hay. "Gabe!" I plead, breathlessly.

"What?" he snaps, irritably.

"It's not what you think," I insist.

162

He shakes his head and grumbles, "It doesn't matter. It's not like you're my girlfriend or anything," he declares, his sarcasm thick.

"Gabe," I beg, "he slipped and I tried to help him. He grabbed me. I fell. We both fell. That's it," I emphasize, desperate for him to understand.

"You don't have to explain yourself," he claims, as his eyes narrow accusingly at me.

"Why are you so angry?" I question, demanding an answer.

He picks up a bale of hay and throws it into the wheelbarrow, harder than necessary causing it to land with a loud thump. "I'm not angry," he grumbles.

I huff a humorless laugh and mumble, "You clearly are."

He stops and stares at me, breathing heavily with his jaw clenched. He finally challenges me, "And so what if I am?"

"I don't understand," I murmur, my voice shaking.

He shakes his head in disbelief. "You have no idea, do you?" he prods, his eyes pleading for an answer.

"Idea of what?" I probe, my eyebrows drawn down in confusion.

He gestures towards me, looking completely vulnerable. "What is it going to take to get you to notice me?" he inquires.

My heart skips a beat and I gasp, "What?" I always notice him. What does he mean? I don't understand.

"Some stranger comes in from the city and you end up wrapped up in his arms for everyone to see," he contests, shaking his head with displeasure.

"Gabe it was an accident," I reiterate. "Why are you so upset?" I repeat, defensively.

He huffs a humorless laugh and shakes his head with incredulity. "Why am I so upset?" he echoes, vehemently. He pauses and looks me in the eyes, glaring at me, causing me to feel it all the way to my soul. He scrunches his face up in frustration just be for he adamantly yells, "Hope, I've never been enough for you!"

My mouth drops open and my eyes widen in shock, as I feel the power of his outburst, almost like he took my heart in his bare hands and crushed it. "Gabe," I gasp.

"It doesn't matter," he grumbles, brushing me off. He shakes his head, appearing devastated. "You're just never going to look at me like that," he states, as if it's a sad fact.

"Like what?" I question, pushing him to explain. I'm still confused, but I feel desperate to understand. I don't want to assume anything, especially not when it comes to us.

"Like more than some guy helping out at the ranch. More than the boy or the kid down the street you grew up with. More than just your friend," he explains, sounding heartbroken. He pauses and takes a deep breath as he places his hands on his hips, appearing resigned. "You know," he begins, "I always thought that you and I were going to end up together down the line," he admits. Then he shakes his head as if that were the most ridiculous idea he's ever had and meets my gaze. "I guess you just don't see us that way," he finishes, looking pained.

My mouth drops open and my heart drops into the pit of my stomach. I stand, momentarily dumbstruck, as Gabe pushes past me with the wheelbarrow full of hay. I gulp down the lump in my throat and I'm finally able to answer, even though he can no longer hear me. "You never asked," I whisper, hoarsely. I close my eyes, uselessly fighting tears, as one slips by without my consent. I feel completely overwhelmed with emotion that I can barely breathe. I hold my hands to my chest, as if it will help hold my heart together and keep me from falling apart. He did feel the same way about me all along. I can't believe it.

Chapter 20

Ethan

I walk through the front door of the inn and immediately spot Frank in the back of the entryway, under the stairs. He has his back to me while he writes daily activities on an eighteen inch by twenty-four inch chalkboard, propped up on a wooden easel. I glance over his shoulder to read the list as he finishes, remembering Amanda saying the ranch has all kinds of special things planned for the holidays. I smile as I read the various activities:

Saturday: Making Ornaments
Sunday: Tree Decorating
Monday: Cookie Exchange
Tuesday: Build a Gingerbread House
Wednesday: Ugly Sweater Party
Thursday: Christmas Cocktails
Friday: Annual Tree Lighting Ceremony

He reaches the bottom of the chalkboard, before I approach him to say Hello. "Hi, Frank," I murmur, smiling down at him, still bent over.

He stands to his full height before he turns around to greet me. "Well, hello there, Ethan. Are you enjoying yourself?" he inquires.

I nod my head in acknowledgement. "I really am. I never knew that a place like this existed in New York," I admit.

A look of what I think is adoration for the ranch crosses his face and he nods his head in agreement. "It's a hidden treasure, that's for sure," he reveals.

I grin at the obvious pride he has for this place. "You can say that again," I agree. "Do you mind if I use it as the setting in my book?" I request.

He nods his head, instantly agreeing. "By all means!" he proclaims. "Maybe we'll get some more business from some of your fans," he adds.

"Maybe," I concur.

"Speaking of fans," he begins and smirks. "How did your riding lesson with Hope go?" he probes, curiously.

I chuckle at the reminder of my lesson, before I tell him the truth. "It was great, until I fell," I concede.

"Fell?" he questions, anxiously; his voice suddenly laced with worry. "Did you get hurt or anything?" he prods.

I shake my head, still smiling and admit, "No, just my pride." I look around into the nearby rooms, checking for signs anyone else might be around, but I don't find the one I'm really looking for. "Where's Joy?" I finally ask.

"She's leading trail rides all day," he informs me. I grimace; disappointed I can't see her now. "She should be back in an hour or so," he adds, as an afterthought.

"Okay," I acknowledge, instantly feeling lighter. "I'm going to head up to my room and write for a bit. Do you mind telling her?" I request.

"Not at all," he agrees.

"Thanks," I murmur, appreciatively.

"Any time," he offers.

I walk out of the foyer, rounding the staircase and climbing up the stairs to my room, while Frank turns back to assess his work on the chalkboard. I stride down to the end of the hallway, my mind already running away with an idea for my next chapter. I turn the key and step into my room, closing the door behind me. I drop the key on the dresser to the left as I walk in. I slip out of my coat and hang it up behind the door on a hook. Then I stride right over to the desk, pull out the wooden chair and sit down. I flip my laptop open and with the document already open, I begin typing, continuing right where I left off. Only this time, I feel as if the story is beginning to tell itself. It's freeing to have the urge or the passion inside me to write again. I already have the story and the characters building inside my head. Now, I just have to get it down before it slips away.

Gabe

I step out of Ashley's stall, an Arabian horse with a long nose and bay in color, or brown with a black tail and mane. She can be playful, but also stubborn, but I'm not in the mood for either today. I make my way over to Nala's stall, a seven-year-old American Paint horse with beautiful brown and white markings. I continue to muck the stalls, raking and cleaning up all the waste, but barely thinking about what I'm doing. I can't get my mind away from Hope and how much the jealousy ate at my insides when I saw her on the ground with Ethan. I heave a sigh and lean on the rake, wondering what she's doing now. She's probably in the kitchen, since she finished feeding the horses so early. I think she said she was making cookies today, but after our conversation, or my rant, I don't think I should go anywhere near that kitchen.

I sigh heavily and quickly finish the last stall. I think I just need to cut out early tonight and figure out what I'm going to do. Last night I thought we were going to kiss and today I find her in the arms of another man. And she has the audacity to ask why I'm so angry? How does she not know? I grimace the moment I realize she knows now and she's still nowhere around me. Instead, she's busy taking care of the guests, just like she always does.

My heart clenches painfully, finally knowing where I stand with her and knowing it's the opposite of what I want. I've been the one who has been there for her all these years. It's exactly where I wanted to be. After everything, I thought it was finally our time to be together. I guess I was wrong. I suddenly feel like such a fool. An image of her and Ethan on the ground flashes through my mind and I flinch, feeling like everything is literally crashing and burning around me. "What am I going to do?" I mutter.

I shake my head and walk over to put all the supplies away. The minute I finish, I reach for my cell phone and call Frank, knowing I need to avoid going near the inn tonight and accidentally running into Hope, if at all possible. He picks up on the first ring. "Hi, Frank. It's Gabe," I announce, even though I'm sure he already checked his caller ID.

He chuckles and asks, "Everything okay?"

I nod, even though he can't see me and clear my throat before I speak. "Yeah," I reply, my voice raspy. "I have everything cleaned up out here and the horses are all fed," I inform him. "Do you mind if I go home early tonight?" I request.

"Of course, Gabe," he agrees. "Eddie is here to put the horses back in the stables later tonight," he reminds me.

"Thanks," I murmur.

"You're not going to stay for dinner tonight?" he questions. "We're just about to eat," he enlightens me. "We all know Hope cooked something delicious," he adds, attempting to entice me to stay. It's not going to work this time, not when she's the very person I'm trying to avoid.

I wince at the mention of Hope, my heart aching and spreading to the rest of my body like a disease. I didn't realize it was already time for dinner. I take a deep breath and attempt to gulp down the lump in my throat. Then I simply inform him, "Thanks, but I can't tonight."

"Okay," he easily relents, without asking any more questions. "Thanks, Gabe and have a good night," he proclaims, thankfully oblivious to my current state of mind.

"Bye," I mumble and quickly end the call, before I decide to say too much.

I close my eyes and take another deep breath and exhale slowly, before opening them. I walk out of the barn and glance up at the inn, imagining Hope standing in front of the stove, looking beautiful as always. The last thing I need right now is to see her, or even eat her cooking. All of it reminds me of something I will never really have. I cringe, my whole body aching at the thought of not having her in my life like I always imagined. I turn away from the inn and stride for my truck before I change my mind. Going inside will only hurt me more. Space from Hope is exactly what I need right now, even if it's never something that I truly want. I climb in behind the wheel and buckle my seat belt. I start my truck and back out of the driveway, heading home, refusing to allow myself even one more glance in the rearview mirror.

Hope

I force a smile as I serve all the guests, including Ethan, who can't seem to take his eyes off of Joy. Then again, her eyes seem to be glued playfully in his direction as well. My heart feels heavy, knowing Gabe already left the ranch for the night, without even saying goodbye. Dad said he just asked to go home early. He almost always eats here and this is the second time he missed dinner this week. As I pass by Ethan's table, he stops me with a concerned gaze. He looks up at me from his chair and questions, "Are you ok, Hope?"

I square my shoulders and paste another smile on my face, even though I know it doesn't reach my eyes. I guess he can see more than my sister, but then again, maybe that's the writer in him. "I'm just tired," I claim, offering him a lame excuse.

He nods his head and narrows his eyes, giving me a look, telling me he doesn't believe me. "Okay," he mumbles, dragging out the word. My eyebrows draw down in puzzlement, but he just shakes his head, thankfully dropping it. "This is delicious," he compliments me. "Thank you," he proclaims, appreciatively. Then he takes another bite of the chicken and rice I made for dinner, another one of my mom's recipes.

I paste on another smile and nod my head in acknowledgement, before I move on to the next table of guests. I feel like all I can do at this point is keep moving like I always have. The repetition and hard work keep my hands and head occupied, most of the time anyway. But with Gabe forcing his way into my thoughts, I'm not quite sure how to handle it, especially when I feel like I already failed him. What could I even do now anyway? I just stood there saying nothing. I already hurt him. I push away my questions and stride back into the kitchen, knowing taking care of the guests for dinner is something I have to get done. I can't exactly let everyone go hungry. Gabe will have to wait. It's not like he wants to talk to me anyway. He's been avoiding me like a pro.

I begin preparing all the completed dishes for dessert, including cookies, brownies, pies and cakes. We always have a wide variety of treats and at this time of year, especially, we really go all out.

I finish setting up all the dessert platters for the guests, with Joy by my side. Then, the moment we're finished, she pulls a chair up next to Ethan without another word to me. She's obviously a bit preoccupied with him. I watch momentarily as she starts chatting with him, her whole face lighting up as they talk. He grins back at her, his eyes sparkling as he watches her with a look of pure wonder. A small, genuine smile touches my lips seeing her so happy and she seems to be having the same affect on him. I rearrange some of the desserts yet again, just for something to keep my hands busy. Then, I turn back to Joy, observing them for a few more minutes before Joy stands and waves to him, giving him a flirtatious smile. His cheeks turn pink as he returns the gesture. Then he stands and walks out of the room, with a quick wave in my direction.

Joy turns and swiftly approaches me, appearing giddy. "Where's he going?" I prompt.

"He wants to go up to his room to work on his writing," she enlightens me. "Since that is the reason he came here, I guess I have to let the man work," she jokes.

I barely have the energy for another smile, but I make sure to have one for Joy. She deserves to be happy. I want that for her and I always want to show her my love and support for whatever or whoever makes her happy, no matter what I'm going through at the time. I nod my head in understanding and murmur, "Good idea." She laughs in response.

I turn and immediately start to clean up the dirty dishes, already scattered on the now empty tables from dessert. I'm desperate to keep my hands busy, until I'm finally able to go to sleep. The only problem is that this time, even keeping myself busy isn't keeping Gabe out of my head. I'm so used to seeing him all over the ranch as I work, but he's been evading me since we talked earlier and then he left early, not even eating dinner with us, like usual. Plus, that conversation keeps running through my head, along with the look of betrayal and devastation on his face as he walked up. I just can't get it out of my mind and it hurts every single time, as if he's shredding my heart before he stomps it into oblivion.

Thinking about his rant, I wonder if it's already too late for us, when I didn't even know we were a real possibility. The thought that it's over before it could even begin causes me to feel as if my heart is breaking over and over again. I take another deep breath and exhale slowly to calm myself down. I give myself a mental shake and mumble under my breath, "I have to stop." Then I force myself to keep moving, just like I always do.

Chapter 21

Hope

Yesterday feels like a complete blur, and yet every minute dragged by so painfully. Every time I tried to catch Gabe's attention or just talk to him, he'd glare at me and turn away. His looks are filled with pain, betrayal, disappointment and regret. It's the opposite of the way I want him to look at me and it feels like a punch in my stomach with every glance in my direction. Every time I see him, my heart feels like it's breaking a little more, causing me to wince just thinking about it.

Yesterday, when I first saw him, he had just finished feeding Loki, a bay colored Thoroughbred from the Seabiscuit bloodline. He was walking by with a bucket in each hand, making his way over to feed Dot, a chestnut colored Arabian with a white stripe down her nose. I was locking up Charley's gate and I couldn't help but smile. Just seeing Gabe has always brought a smile to my face. I can't help it, but his reaction to seeing me was the opposite of our normal. His eyes dropped to the ground, a wrinkle formed in his brow and he stalked away from me, without any kind of acknowledgement. His actions caused my heart to lodge itself in my throat. Then a tingly ache, started in my throat and spread to all my limbs. I leaned against the fence by Charley's gate and watched him walk away as I fought back tears. I had to take a couple deep breaths to calm myself down, before forcing myself to return my attention to readying the horses.

The rest of the day was much of the same; with Gabe doing everything he could to avoid me. I wanted to keep myself busy, but I let Joy handle all of the Christmas activities. I know I can't avoid everything, but I just couldn't fake happiness around the guests. I'm just not feeling very festive. Joy helped dad finish decorating the lobby, while I gave Ethan another riding lesson, during his break from writing. This time he rode Jayne, a bay colored Arabian. Joy also led the guests in making Christmas tree ornaments last night. Then again, Joy has always been the outgoing one anyway. She enjoys doing the crafts and other activities with the guests. I could hear her laughing and having fun with everyone, whenever I walked by the dining area. I heave a sigh, wishing today was better, but so far its been the same as yesterday. I'm just not really sure what I can do to make everything okay with Gabe, but that's all I want.

Now, I stand outside, taking everything in, including the Christmas tree we wouldn't even have if it weren't for Gabe. He seems to be in everything around here and I wish it could remain that way. I glance around at all the guests from the inn, including Ethan, along with local family, friends and neighbors, decorating the Christmas tree and the hay bales Gabe and Ethan set up. My heart feels heavy with Gabe's absence.

I try to keep to myself and take my time decorating to avoid Joy asking me any questions, but I'm not so lucky. Out of the corner of my eye I see her approaching, with clear determination in her eyes, and a candy cane sticking out of her mouth. "Where's Gabe?" she immediately inquires, without a greeting.

I grimace and grumble my response without looking at her. "I don't know."

175

She sighs dramatically and shakes her head in disappointment. "Hope, What is going on between you two?" she asks, demanding an answer.

I flinch and quietly admit, "It's a long story."

She covers my hand with hers to stop me from decorating the tree. I slowly lift my head to look her in the eyes, anticipating her words. "Fix it," she stresses, leaving little room for argument.

I try anyway and innocently question, "Fix what?"

She arches her eyebrows in challenge. "Come on, Sis," she prods. "Something had to have happened between you two. This is the first year in," she pauses thinking, before continuing, "I don't even know how long, that Gabe isn't decorating the tree with us," she emphasizes. I look down at the ground, hating that he's not here, but it's my fault. I'm just not sure what to say. She continues, not waiting for me to speak. "You don't have to tell me what happened, but you do need to find him and fix whatever broke," she asserts.

"I don't know what broke," I claim, weakly.

She narrows her eyes at me and insists, "I don't believe you."

My eyes widen and my mouth drops open, as my head snaps back to hers in shock. "Excuse me?" I question, my disbelief clear.

"Look," she begins, "anyone can see that you love him and he loves you," she insists.

I have a quick intake of breath, my heart filling with hope. I look her in the eyes and prompt, "Do you really think so?"

She grins wide and confirms, "I know so. No other guy would do what he has done for you, protect you the way he has and been there for you if he wasn't in love," she proclaims. She crosses her arms over her chest and arches her eyebrows, daring me to refute her statement.

I take a deep breath, gathering my thoughts. Then I gulp down the lump in my throat and quietly admit, "I don't know how to fix this."

She shrugs as if the answer is obvious. "Tell him," she announces.

"What?" I prod.

"You need to find him and tell him exactly what you're thinking. Tell him what's in your heart," she clarifies.

"Now?" I question, suddenly anxious.

"Right now," she maintains. "He should be with us, Hope. He's family," she affirms.

She's right. He should be here and he is family. Except the way I see him fitting in with our family is probably much different than it is for Joy and maybe that's always been part of the problem. I was afraid to speak up because I didn't want to lose what we have, but now it seems I might have lost him anyway. I have that same feeling I always have in my heart when it comes to Gabe. I can't sit here and wait for him to stop avoiding me before I talk to him; that could be too late. I need to tell him how I feel. A small smile tugs at my lips and I nod my head in agreement. I look at my sister and concede, "You're right."

She grins, obviously enjoying those words, but I'm grateful she doesn't make a joke. Instead, she prompts, "Do you know where he is?"

I nod my head in acknowledgement, my smile slowly growing. "I have a good idea," I claim.

I turn and make my escape towards the barn, as Ethan approaches Joy. My stride becomes quicker, as my determination grows. I take a step inside the barn and breathe a sigh of relief the moment I spot Gabe, grateful he's still here. He has Sport tethered, while he brushes him. I lick my lips, my mouth suddenly dry, knowing what I need to say to him. I open my mouth and force myself to speak before I lose my courage. "I knew I'd find you in here," I announce.

He turns around and glances at me without a reaction, before he spins back around, wordlessly, continuing to brush Sport, methodically. I take a deep breath and exhale slowly, hating how hard everything is between us right now. "Are you really not going to talk to me?" I prompt, my voice cracking with my pain.

He untethers Sport and takes his time, guiding him back into his stall. "What do you want me to say?" he grumbles, keeping his back to me.

"Gabe, look at me," I plead. He refuses to turn around, making me wince. He steps out of the stall and closes it. I raise my voice slightly and desperately repeat, "Look at me!"

He spins around to face me with wide eyes, obviously surprised by my demand. "What?" he solicits.

I hold his gaze and say the words I tried to say the other night, but couldn't get out of my mouth before he walked away. "You never asked," I state, answering his question from days ago.

"What?" he prompts, obviously puzzled by my statement.

"You...Never...Asked," I repeat, saying each word clearly and pausing for emphasis.

"Asked what?" he reiterates.

I feel the anger inside of me bubbling to a boil. "If I saw us together down the line," I answer. I pause for breath, before I continue. "You have no right to get angry with me because of what you saw. You were right about one thing, Gabriel Corsetti. I'm not your girlfriend. And do you know why?" I question and wait for him to respond.

His eyes soften and he smirks, clearly amused with my outburst. Then he asks, "Why?"

"Because you never asked," I repeat. "I was helping Ethan learn to ride so he could go on the trails with Joy. Eddie had just taken Cupcake away when Ethan slipped in the mud. When he fell, he grabbed me and I fell on top of him. I don't know what you think you saw, but you are dead wrong," I inform him, vehemently. "I don't look at any other guy, but you, Gabe," I proclaim, my heart racing with my admission. "I always," I emphasize, "saw us together down the line. I have loved you my entire life," I confess. "When my mom died, you were the person that was only there for me. I haven't stepped foot off this ranch in five years, and when I did the other day, it was with you, because I felt safe with you. No one else, Gabriel," I insist. "You," I reiterate.

As I finish my rant, I finally begin to register the relieved and confident smile that covers his face, as his whole body relaxes with my confession. He takes a step towards me and looks me in the eyes, his own eyes sparkling. Then he declares, "I know."

"Do you?" I prod, defiantly. "I'm sorry if I don't wear my heart on my sleeve, or don't say what I'm feeling. You, of all people, know more than anyone else how I've been since I watched my mother and my aunt get killed right in front of me. It's something that's going to affect me for the rest of my life! I don't care if it was five years ago! I thought you, above all people would understand that," I proclaim.

He visibly flinches and steps closer to me, stopping right in front of me. "Hope, I do," he contends. "But you need to cut me some slack," he requests. "I've never asked for anything in return. Ever," he emphasizes.

"I know that," I concede.

"I have waited my whole life to hear you say that you love me," he admits, reverently, causing my heart to skip a beat. He reaches out and grasps both of my hands in his. He looks deep into my eyes, causing my breath to catch in my throat. "I love you, Hope. I always have," he confesses, with genuine vulnerability.

I gasp, my heart instantly mended and ready to jump into his arms with his words. "You have?" I prompt, my voice barely a squeak.

He chuckles softy and shakes his head, as if I should know better than to even ask. He nods his head and proclaims, "Yes. I was on my way the day of the accident, but, well," he murmurs and then he grimaces. He continues, his voice gentle, "The accident changed everything."

I cast my eyes downward, my heart heavy. Then I acknowledge, "I changed."

He leans down and waits until I meet his gaze again. His eyes fill with something I can't quite name, but it causes my heart to skip a beat. "We all did. But my feelings for you didn't. Not once," he maintains. "I don't care if you never want to leave the ranch again," he claims. "As long as I'm here with you," he states.

The corners of my mouth curve upwards as my heartbeat quickens. "Really?" I prompt.

He grins and nods in confirmation, "Yes. You don't want to ride anymore, that's fine. You don't have to. Heck, you can stay in the kitchen and bake cookies all day, that's fine," he proclaims, a smile tugging at his lips. "I love you for you, Hope. Nothing will ever change that," he emphasizes. "I've been carrying this with me for a long time," he murmurs, the intensity in his gaze, giving me chills.

"I've been carrying it, too," I reveal, smiling up at him.

He chuckles softly and shakes his head. "Not that, Hope. This," he states. He reaches his thumb and pointer finger into a small, hidden pocket on the right side of his jeans and pulls out an engagement ring. My hand flies to cover my mouth, as I gasp in shock. "It was my grandma's," he informs me, a shy smile on his lips. "I've had it in my pocket since the night of the accident, when I was bringing it to you as a promise. But, I guess it has more meaning now." He lowers himself to one knee and looks up at me, holding the ring in his hand and bringing tears to my eyes. He smiles and proclaims, "Hope, I promise you that I will always be there for you. I promise to protect and take care of you. I promise that I will always be by your side, no matter what. I promise that I will be the best husband that I can ever be."

My heart pounds erratically, while a tingling sensation takes over my insides. "Oh, Gabe," I rasp, clasping my hands to my chest, attempting to get them to stop shaking.

He holds the ring a little closer to me as he officially proposes, "Hope Lindsay McGregor, will you be my wife? Will you marry me?"

I nod my head emphatically and hold my left hand out to him. He slips the ring on my finger and smiles proudly. "What took you so long?" I tease.

He stands up and wraps me in his arms. I let my hands rest on his arms as he finally presses his soft lips to mine, without hesitation; in a kiss we've both been waiting for way too long. It's a kiss where the rest of the world falls away and no one else exists in our little bubble except for Gabe and me. I pull back for a breath, letting my forehead rest against his, feeling overwhelmed with happiness and love.

He looks down at me grinning from ear to ear. "Do you want to go tell your family?" he inquires.

"In a minute," I mumble. Then, I tilt my head back to him and kiss him one more time, loving the warm feeling that spreads throughout my whole body as our lips move in perfect rhythm, before we break apart again. "I love you, Gabe," I rasp, needing to say the words again and needing him to hear them. I know this is exactly where I'm supposed to be.

"I love you too," he whispers. After another moment in his arms, he insists, "Come on, we need to tell your dad."

I giggle and add, "And Joy." He grasps my hand, lacing our fingers together. He holds my hand up to look at the ring on my finger and smiles, proudly, making my heart feel full again. Then he drops our hands between us, as we stride out of the barn together.

As we approach everyone still decorating by the tree, Joy's gaze immediately goes to our joined hands before she looks at me with wide eyes and a huge smile. I nearly bounce in excitement as I pull my hand away from his to hold it up for her to see. She screeches in excitement and throws her arms around me. "Now that's how you fix things," she declares, making me laugh. I cling to my sister, feeling a lump form in my throat. I squeeze her tightly, truly happy. When she releases me, Ethan offers his congratulations and I notice my dad approaching us out of the corner of my eye, trying to find out what all the commotion is about from all of us.

I look at him, emotion still think on my tongue and hold up my hand to answer his question with a permanent smile on my face. I think I see happy tears in his eyes, just before he picks me up and hugs me tightly. "Congratulations, Sweetheart. I'm so happy for you two. Your mom would be too," he whispers. I gasp, barely holding back my own tears, at his mention of mom.

Dad reluctantly releases me and turns towards Gabe. He congratulates him, patting him on the back, in a one-armed hug. He releases Gabe and turns to the crowd. Then he loudly broadcasts, "Hope and Gabe are engaged!"

Cheers erupt all around us. Then our friends, family and neighbors, suddenly surround both Gabe and me, offering us congratulations. The rest of the night feels like it passes by in a blur, but it's one I don't ever want to forget.

Chapter 22

Joy

Hope and I finish cleaning up from building Gingerbread houses with some of the guests and set up in our kitchen to make ours at the same time. My favorite part of doing ours after all of the guests are done, is we get to use all the left over candy and frosting. That way I'm able to nibble on whatever I want as we work. I make my way into the kitchen with the last of the supplies and find Hope with tubes of frosting, candy, and the gingerbread pieces needed to put the house together already spread out for us on the far end of the kitchen table, next to our old fashioned popcorn machine. "I'm all done in the dining room," I announce.

"Excellent!" she exclaims. She glances up at me and grins. "Want to work on ours now?" she requests, pure excitement in her voice.

"Absolutely!" I confirm.

I walk over and sit down at the end of the table next to Hope. I pick up one of the tubes of white frosting and squirt a little bit of on the tip of my finger. I glance at my sister as I eat the frosting off my finger, but she doesn't notice. She's too busy attempting to use the same frosting from her own tube to glue the sides of the house together. "We should wait to glue the roof on until we decorate all the sides," she instructs. "That will give the sides time to dry so they don't fall over from the weight of it. Be careful, though," she warns me.

I grin in response, since I'm usually the one doing most of the craft projects. But we both helped the guests with the project today. Everyone always enjoys this one, especially the kids. Hope excels at projects involving any kind of food and she enjoys taking the lead for ones like this. I'm happy to let her, but making Gingerbread houses is something I definitely want to help with. It tastes too good and it's always so much fun. Besides, watching her today is so different than normal. She has her hair pulled up in a high ponytail to keep it out of her face, but it just helps me see her grin. She hasn't wiped that smile off her face for even a second and I love it. She's been through so much. We all have, but Hope even more. She deserves to be happy and I honestly haven't seen her like this since I left for college...since before the accident. I'm not going to take a moment of this time for granted.

I add frosting and then I add red and green candies to the sides, eating a few in between, before I start getting impatient. "Can we add the roof now?" I request.

She bursts out laughing, but relents. "Okay," she agrees, nodding her head. She stops and pushes up the sleeves of her dark blue and white flannel shirt before she grabs both pieces of the roof and places them in front of her. She lines the top of the house on one side with frosting and places a roof piece gently on top, while I support the sides. Then, she repeats the process, adding the next piece. Next, she adds frosting along the break between the two pieces on top. We both support the pieces for a minute before she hesitantly announces, "That should hold it." We both slowly release the house and it thankfully doesn't even waver. She grins proudly and then we both reach for a decorator tube full of frosting.

Ethan strides into the kitchen looking incredibly handsome, comfortable and ready for a day at the ranch. He's wearing jeans like Hope and me, along with a gray t-shirt and a dark green and navy flannel draped over it. I glance down at my long sleeved white shirt, adorned with red and black, plaid, long-sleeves and my puffy navy vest, trying to make sure I don't have any frosting on me before I meet his gaze. He greets us both with a broad smile. "Hi Joy. Hi Hope."

"Hi," Hope replies.

"Hey, Ethan," I murmur, casually. I reach up and push my long curls back over my shoulder and out of the way of the frosting. "Where'd you escape to last night?" I question.

"I was working," he states.

"Writing," I mumble, my voice thick with sarcasm. Writing doesn't seem like work to me. I enjoy it way too much for it to feel like work.

He smirks, obviously amused. "Well, that is what I do," he remarks.

I shrug, like its no big deal, but I'll admit to myself that I think it's amazing. I honestly admire how hard he works and what he does for a living. Who doesn't want a job where they do what they love? "So do you want to help us make our gingerbread house?" I inquire, as my way of inviting him to join Hope and me.

He grins and instantly accepts, "I'd love to."

"Great!" I declare.

"I thought I missed this," he adds.

"Well, technically you did," I smirk. "We just finished up making the houses in the dining room with all the guests. This one is just for us," I explain.

"Are you sure you two want me to help then?" he prompts.

I nod my head in confirmation. "Come on," I encourage, with a playful smile in his direction. I scoot my chair over, moving closer to Hope, seated on the bench at the kitchen table to make more room for him in front of the gingerbread house. We do all need room to work on the same house, I think to myself, knowing it's an excuse to have him close, but I don't care. Ethan sits down on my other side, giving me goosebumps at his close proximity.

"So what do we do first?" he asks.

"Here," Hope mumbles, as she offers him a decorator's tube filled with green frosting.

He takes it from her and murmurs, "Thanks."

"Now we decorate," I announce. He watches as I start decorating the roof with white frosting, while Hope begins accenting the windows on the sides. I glance over at him and playfully question, "Are you going to help?"

He chuckles and works on the opposite side from Hope. I put a little frosting on my finger and put my finger in my mouth, instantly licking off the sweet taste. Ethan laughs, garnering Hope's attention, "Joy," she scolds, not intimidating me with her smile. I offer her a shrug, since this is just the first time she caught me today. Then I squirt a small amount of frosting onto the back of her hand, making her jump in her seat. I giggle at her reaction. Then I turn and purposely put frosting on Ethan's nose, wanting to see what he'll do.

He laughs and pretends to be mad, "Hey!" Then he leans towards me and swiftly streaks frosting along my cheek. I burst out laughing and look back at him, smiling back at me, his hazel eyes sparkling with a touch of gold.

"Are you two going to even pretend to decorate this gingerbread house with me?" Hope teases. Ethan blushes, causing my heart to skip a beat. Then my heart refills and overflows, enjoying his reaction.

"Oh, I guess we can try," I joke. I smile at Ethan, as if he's the only one I see, before turning back to our project. We all continue to put frosting and candies on the house, attempting to make it look beautiful and festive. I use green candies to add a wreath on the front door. Hope uses mini pretzel twists to add a picket fence and then drizzles it with white frosting for snow. Then she adds green candied leaves with red berries on a pretzel rod topped with a gumdrop for a light post. Ethan uses marshmallows to make a snowman in the front, making me laugh. It seems I can't stop flirting with this man, but he doesn't seem to mind, returning my gestures and I love it.

It seems time moved much too quickly, when Hope suddenly stands up and announces, "I think it looks pretty good."

I nod in agreement, although I'm sad we're done. "My part looks good anyway," I tease. Both Hope and Ethan laugh in response and I quickly amend my statement, relenting to the truth. "I guess we all did a pretty good job," I concede, rolling my eyes dramatically.

Hope grins wide and shakes her head in amusement. She strolls towards the window looking out towards one of the stables, while she admires her engagement ring. When she reaches the window she looks outside and spots someone, who I assume is Gabe. She smiles even wider if that's possible and waves to him adoringly. Not for the first time today, emotion builds up in my chest, feeling as if it's about to bubble over into my throat. Seeing her so happy is doing so many wonderful things for our whole family, including Gabe, of course. She spins around, turning away from the window. Then she cheerfully broadcasts, "I'm going to go outside and talk to Gabe."

I nod my head in acknowledgement and mumble, "Okay."

Ethan adds, "Have fun."

She practically bounces to the door, her happiness emanating from every part of her. It's almost like she's a different person, no, I shake my head, stopping my thought. She's not a different person, it's almost like we have the old Hope back now that she has everything figured out with Gabe. I watch as she pulls her boots on and pulls the sliding glass door open. She steps outside with her eyes already on Gabe and pushes the door shut behind her.

Then I turn my attention back to Ethan. "What's your plan for the rest of the day?" I ask, hoping to spend more time with him.

"Well," he begins, "I do have to get some more work done on my book, but I was wondering if you would like to go to the 'Ugly Sweater Party' with me tomorrow night?" he inquires, the corners of his mouth curving upwards.

My eyes widen in surprise. He obviously knows I'm planning on going, but he wants me to go with him. My heartbeat feels as if it's suddenly out of control. I take a deep breath and look up at him from underneath my eyelashes, feigning calm. I smile and agree, "I'd like that."

A relieved smile consumes his face, his eyes sparkling. "Great," he murmurs. I momentarily get lost in his gaze. It feels as if I'm under a spell as I stare into his eyes. No, not just under a spell, his spell. "Well, thank you for letting me help with your gingerbread house. I really had a lot of fun," he proclaims.

I clear my throat and admit, "Me too. And you're welcome," I add. "I should probably let you get back to your writing," I mumble, begrudgingly. "I have some things I have to get ready for the party tomorrow anyway," I add. I need to walk away and pull myself together. He just caught me by surprise when he asked me out. "I'll see you later?" I reiterate.

"I'll see you later, Joy," he confirms. Then, I watch him walk out of the kitchen, until he disappears around the corner near the stairs, heading up to his room.

"Bye," I call after him. I stand and begin cleaning up all the supplies from decorating the gingerbread house, knowing I owe Hope for all the times she cleaned up for me. Then I walk by the front lobby and stop when I notice dad standing at the fireplace. He's adding another Christmas stocking, alongside the rest of ours. I quietly take a step a little closer, slightly confused. Then I see Gabe's name on the top of the red and white stocking and smile to myself. Everything is finally turning around for the McGregor family.

I continue on to the office and glance out the window, noticing a blur of color. I stop and look outside, seeing Hope and Gabe. I don't even bother hiding that I'm watching the two of them laughing together, but they don't notice me anyway. They're too wrapped up in each other, just as it should be. She steps towards him and wraps her arms around his waist. My heart feels full watching how happy they are together. It's been way too long since I've truly seen that look on her face and I'm incredibly grateful for it. I huff a laugh and admit to myself, I'm thankful to Gabe for helping to put it there. She deserves it. "It's about time," I reiterate, happily.

I lift the top off a red and green storage bin and peak inside, finding the things I'm looking for without much effort. I replace the lip and pick up the box of Christmas decorations from behind the desk and bring them back over into the gathering room by the fireplace. "Hi, Dad," I greet him, announcing my presence, as I set the container down. "I have a few more finishing touches for the Christmas tree and this room for the party tomorrow night. Do you want to help me?" I request.

"I'd love to, Sweetheart," he instantly agrees. He lifts the top of the bin and I immediately pull out the silver and gold angel tree topper. My dad looks down at it in admiration. "Your mom loved that angel," he murmurs, softly.

I nod in agreement, a memory clear in my mind from a Christmas long ago when my mom came home with the angel. Then I prompt, "Would you help me?" We work together to put the angel on top of the tree, before we add other decorations to the tree as well as around the room. I plug in the lights to test them and hold my hand up to dad for a high five, but he fists his hand making it awkward, like only he can. I smirk and he just chuckles and shrugs in response.

"I'll have Gabe set up the tables for us before he leaves for the night," Dad acknowledges.

"Would you like me to put the rest of the bins away?" I ask.

Ethan walks into the room and offers, "If you need something put away, I can help. I need a break," he informs us.

"Thank you," I tell him, accepting his offer. I watch as he helps my dad carry the bins back to the office to put away in the closet. My heart clenches seeing him helping my dad and I bring my hand to my chest. I'm amazed a little more by Ethan every time I see him.

Chapter 23

Joy

The next day flies by. I kept busy with three trail rides, all with different guests, our trail dog, Heidi, running alongside nearly all day. She's a chestnut colored Rottweiler and Australian Shepherd mix with a lot of energy. She's actually one of our ranch hand's dogs and she loves to run the trails with the horses when she's here. After my scheduled rides, I helped Hope set up for the Ugly Sweater party tonight. But the whole time I couldn't stop thinking about my upcoming date with Ethan. It feels as if no time has passed since I saw him last night, at the same time it feels like time has dragged by, while I wait for our date. I'm excited and I also feel like I have a nervous energy running through me.

I step up to my full-length mirror to assess myself, before I walk over to his room. I only had a few options for sweaters, but I wanted to wear something that fit the theme, but wasn't too crazy. After all, this is our first date. I'm wearing a burgundy sweater with white polka dots and red reindeer across the top, along with black ripped jeans and short brown boots with a one and a half inch heel. I purse my lips, but I honestly think it's the best I could do with an ugly sweater.

I step out my bedroom door and make my way over to the inn. I wave to my dad standing behind the front desk as I round the corner to head upstairs.

"Where's your sweater, Dad?" I inquire, noticing his plain black shirt.

He chuckles, "Don't worry, Joy. I've got it right here," he enlightens me, nodding behind him. "You're going to get Ethan?" he prompts.

I nod and feel my face heat as I confirm, "Yes. We'll see you in a few minutes."

"Okay," he agrees.

I walk upstairs and stop in front of Ethan's door. I hold my hand up and knock, anxiously waiting for him to answer. I let my eyes sweep over my outfit one more time and grimace. Ethan opens the door and I raise my eyes up to him. "Hi," I begin, but I stop and immediately burst out laughing at the sight in front of me.

"What?" he questions, innocently. "You don't like my sweater?" he probes. "You picked it out for me," he reminds me of what I already know. He obviously didn't pack anything for a party like this, so I helped him out. I gave him a reindeer sweater, like mine, but his is white with black dots everywhere and reindeer in a line across the top, stating "Oh, Deer" repetitively underneath. I think he wins between the two of us.

"You look great," I smirk.

His eyes narrow, but he smiles back at me as he takes me in. He returns the compliment, claiming, "So do you, Joy." The sincerity in his tone causes my cheeks to instantly heat. "Should we go?" he prods.

I nod my head in agreement and mumble, "Yeah."

We walk downstairs and turn into our front gathering room by the fireplace. Everything looks great, with the Christmas tree fully decorated, the stockings hung along the mantel, thick, green garland with red berries and pine cones draped around the windows, Christmas accessories on the built-in bookshelves and accent tables. We used the two long tables Gabe brought in on the other side of the room. We covered them with a white tablecloth, decorated with large red and green poinsettias. Then we filled it with appetizers and desserts served on holiday platters. We also have drinks set up on one end with water and a Christmas punch kids always love, a coffee and tea bar, as well as both red and white wine.

"Wow," Ethan murmurs. "This looks really great," he compliments, as he looks around, taking in our surroundings.

"Thank you," I reply. He looks down at me and brushes my arm with his. Then he lightly grasps my pinkie and ring finger with his fingers, shooting tingles up my arm. "I'm glad you like it," I whisper softly.

"Hi, Joy," one of our long time guests greets me as she walks into the room with her husband. I tear my gaze away from Ethan's and offer her a small wave.

Ethan and I look around the room as people walk in, taking in all the ugly Christmas sweaters. "Some people really go all out, huh?" I ask.

He chuckles softly as we step up behind a young married couple in extremely colorful matching sweaters. They're black with thick stripes of red, green, blue, white and black, all with different patterns wrapped around from front to back, including Ho, Ho, Ho, Christmas trees, snowflakes and festive designs. "I like the matching sweaters," Ethan acknowledges as they turn and walk by.

"Thanks," they reply in unison. "You too," they add, before they continue walking away.

I glance up and see dad across the room, smiling politely at one of our guests wearing a bright green Christmas sweater with a giant Santa face on the front and the top of his hat hangs off as an oversized white ball of fluff. "Let's go say hi to my dad," I suggest. I tug Ethan in his direction. We step up to him, just as the guest walks away. "Nice sweater, Dad," I smirk.

He holds his arms out and grins, showcasing his colorful and very busy, dark red cardigan sweater over the top of his black shirt. The sweater is filled with rows of gingerbread men, Christmas trees, mistletoe, candy canes, presents, tin soldiers, Christmas greetings and more. "I could say the same about the two of you," he teases, nodding towards both of our sweaters. We all burst out laughing in response.

"I think you win this year, though, Dad," I insist.

"Not everyone is here yet," he reminds me.

I point in the direction of the doorway, just as Gabe and Hope walk into the party hand in hand. They both have contagious smiles covering their faces, as they glance at each other and then across the room, spotting all of us. My eyes widen and I laugh even harder. "I was wrong. I think Gabe definitely wins," I announce. Gabe has on a bright green sweater, the arms stitched with strings of lights, while the front has a fireplace with four stuffed mini stockings hanging out of it, like they're hanging off the mantel. While Hope took a milder approach wearing a gray sweater, with accessories forming a Santa face, including a hat, sunglasses, a cherry nose and a large mustache.

"You look great, Guys," I proclaim, as they approach.

Hope glances at Gabe and grins, tugging lightly on one of the stockings. I laugh again and compliment him, "You did great, Gabe." I may be referring to more than the sweater, but I don't say that as we continue talking about the rest of our plans for the holidays. I take a deep breath and exhale slowly, enjoying the feel of my hand enveloped in Ethan's and the pure joy on all our faces; Dad, Hope, Gabe, as well as Ethan and me. As I take it all in, I admit to myself that for the first time since mom died, it really feels like Christmas again.

As the night winds down and guests begin to disperse, I look for another reason to spend more time with Ethan. "Would you like to ride the trails with me tomorrow?" I propose.

"I'd love to," Ethan instantly replies.

I smile and suggest, "We'll go after lunch. That way you can get some writing done before I take up all your time."

He chuckles, but quickly agrees, "Sounds good." Then, as an afterthought he gives my hand a light squeeze and informs me, "For the record, I like when you occupy my time."

I feel my face heat with his compliment and my heart pounds even harder, as if it's trying to break through to reach him. "In that case, we also have a Christmas cocktail party tomorrow night. Would you like to come with me?" I offer.

"I can definitely take a break to come spend time with you," he insists. "I'll be there," he adds.

I smile up at him and open my mouth to reply, just as Hope steps up next to us. "I'm sorry to interrupt, guys," she begins.

"It's okay, I should head back to my room to get some more writing done anyway," Ethan informs her.

Hope grins and replies, "Thanks, Ethan. Then Joy, can you help me clean up the food table?" she requests.

I nod my head in agreement. "Sure," I murmur.

"I'll see you tomorrow?" Ethan requests.

"Absolutely," I confirm. I wave as he rounds the corner, before I turn back to help Hope. She has a mischievous grin on her face and I hold up my hand in warning, "Don't start!"

She laughs as she picks up an empty dessert platter and strides for the kitchen.

Ethan

I close my laptop, satisfied with where I'm leaving off for now. I walk over to the mirror and give myself a quick look. I gently push a few stray hairs back into place and run my hands over my dark green long sleeved shirt, smoothing it out, while I think about my ride on the trails with Joy today. I did better than I expected. The lessons all of them are giving me are really starting to pay off. She rode Twinkle, a chestnut Arabian, while she had me on Kaya, a large black, Quarter horse with a white stripe down her nose. The trails are absolutely beautiful with all the trees, flowers, streams and curves in the land. Plus, at my skill level, I'm sure there's so much more to see that I'm not quite ready for. I followed behind her, as she pointed out different things she thought I might enjoy seeing. More than anything, I enjoyed hearing the sound of her laughter floating back to me. "Well, let's go see her, then," I mumble to myself.

I walk downstairs and find Joy in the gathering room. She sees me walk in and steps up to me with a wide smile. "You made it," she grins.

"You're here," I reply.

"Would you like something to drink?" she inquires. "Eddie is making some Christmas cocktails," she informs me. I glance over to the tables they had set up with food and drinks last night and see Eddie behind it handing a red drink to a little girl in a clear plastic cup decorated with red and green confetti.

"Sure," I agree. I instinctively reach for her hand, entwining my fingers with hers. Her cheeks turn a light

197

shade of pink and I can't help, but smile. It amazes me how she lights up every room she walks into.

As we approach, she begins telling me about the various drinks. "There's a peppermint one, a cranberry one, a Christmas cookie one," she enlightens me.

I chuckle and interrupt her list. "Why don't you surprise me," I suggest.

She smirks and nods her head in agreement. She turns towards the table and requests, "Hi, Eddie, could we have one of the Christmas cookie drinks and the cranberry citrus one?"

"Sure," he agrees.

He quickly makes the drinks and hands them both to Joy. "Thank you," she murmurs. Then she turns to me and offers, "Here, you can try this one first."

I chuckle softly and take a sip of the red drink. "Thank you," I tell her. We walk over towards the fireplace, the flames of the small fire, mesmerizing in their dance. I look up at Joy, her face aglow in the firelight and I can't help, but smile at her beauty. She's wearing a ribbed, ivory, long-sleeved shirt, with an olive green denim vest over it and ripped jeans with dark brown cowboy boots. She styled her long hair in loose curls and let it fall gently over her shoulders, taking my breath away, but I've come to expect it in her presence.

"So how's the writing going?" she inquires.

"I think it's going pretty well," I admit.

"Do you have a name for it yet?" she asks.

"How about this, I'll tell you the name if you share more about yourself with me," I suggest.

"I do share things about me with you," she insists.

He nods, "Yes, but I want to know what you think about at night, or when you're out riding on the horses. I want to know what drives you or gives you inspiration and not the horse," I tease. She smirks and blushes in response, thinking I'm done. But I continue to elaborate. "I want to know what makes you happy or sad. I want to know what makes you laugh and what puts that sparkle in your beautiful blue eyes. I want to know what you like to do for fun and what you like to do to relax. I just want to know you, Joy," I request.

Her eyes widen and she bites her lower lip, hesitating. "That's a lot," she concedes.

I nod my head in agreement and reveal, "We can take as much time as you need and I'm happy to tell you anything you'd like to know." I just really want her to show me a little more of herself. I want her to let me in, even if it's just a small piece at a time. I may want to know everything, but I don't want to push her into it either.

She finally nods her head slowly in response and offers me a small smile, causing my heart to skip a beat. "Okay," she whispers.

I grin wide and softly murmur, "Great!"

She smiles at me and my heart skips a beat. I don't know if I'm going to be ready to leave when it's time to go back to New York. I'd miss her smile way too much. She's just starting to open up and I don't want to miss a moment of it.

Chapter 24

Gabe

I look up and spot my mom and dad walking towards our group, standing outside around the Christmas tree and I smile. I meet them part way to greet them, "Hi, Mom. Hi, Dad." I lean down and wrap my arms around my mom, giving her a quick hug. "I'm glad you guys are here," I convey.

"You know we wouldn't miss it," she reminds me, as she reluctantly releases me. I nod my head in acknowledgement. "Besides your dad looks forward to the hot chocolate every year," she teases him, as the corners of her mouth twitch up in amusement.

He chuckles and arches his eyebrows in challenge. "And you don't?" he prompts. She laughs and waves him off, without answering, just as Frank approaches to greet my parents. "Frank," dad says, announcing his arrival. He reaches his hand out to him and they shake firmly.

"Merry Christmas, Frank," my mom says, and then greets him with a hug. "Everything looks absolutely wonderful," she praises.

He nods his head in agreement. "Thanks, but I have to give most of the credit to my girls and Gabe," he acknowledges.

I shake my head, dismissing his compliment of me. "Hope and Joy should have the credit," I insist.

"Don't let him fool you," Frank maintains. "He's always been a hard worker. Plus, we all know he'll always go the extra mile to help Hope," he adds, grinning proudly. I shrug my shoulders in response, knowing it's true. I'd do anything to make her happy. He turns back to my parents and tells them, "I'm really glad you guys could make it tonight."

I interrupt, before they can continue and inform them, "I'm going to let you guys catch up." They barely acknowledge my comment, already deep in conversation as I step away, making me chuckle. I stuff my hands in the pockets of my chocolate brown winter coat, as I step away from the crowd. I feel like everything is right again for the first time since the accident. I don't think I could wipe the smile from my face if I had to.

While Joy and Ethan were out riding the trails this morning, I spent my time helping Hope in the stables. To me, it's all the little things I'm able to do now, that I've never been able to do before, that makes all the difference. In fact, before I was always so worried about stepping over an invisible boundary, that I held back, when I should have been asking for more. At least now I'm able to enjoy them. The simple things, like our playful banter as we work together, or just talking and laughing, holding her hand, giving her a hug, or a sweet kiss, are my favorite parts of the day. Then again, anything with Hope will always be my favorite. I huff a laugh and give my head a light shake of disbelief. I don't know why it took me so long to tell her how I feel about her. I was so focused on her grieving and being there for her, that I almost let her slip right through my fingers. I'm so grateful we finally figured everything out to bring us to each other. I'm not going to miss another moment to tell her I love her for the rest of my life.

I lean against the fence, perfectly content watching Hope amongst the guests. I'm happy she's wearing her olive green winter coat instead of her familiar jean jacket. Tonight definitely feels more like winter. I keep my eyes on her as she makes her way around the corral, talking to a few of our family, friends, neighbors and guests staying at the inn. Everyone is bundled up in the cold night air, while all of them wait, excited for the tree lighting. One of our teenage neighbors is even bundled up in a Santa suit, alongside their dogs bundled up in Christmas sweaters to keep them warm. I love it. Hope steps away from them and glances up at the dark night sky, the stars now visible and twinkling brightly against the nearly black backdrop. Her smile is the thing that draws me in though. To me, it shines brighter than every single star hanging in the sky. She slowly brings her head back down and looks around the gathering crowd, quickly meeting my gaze. Her eyes sparkle in the moonlight, causing my heart to pick up its pace. I easily return her smile and clear my throat, attempting to dislodge the sudden lump in my throat. I watch as she quickly closes the distance between us. She stops in front of me and inquires, "Are you ready?"

I nod in agreement, "Yeah. Are you?" I question. She nods in confirmation and I hold my hand out to her. She sighs happily as she slips her hand into mine, giving me a burst of adrenaline. I give her hand a loving squeeze, reveling in her squeeze back. We stroll up towards the Christmas tree, opposite the crowd of friends, family and neighbors. I smile at her, grateful to be standing with her for the first time at the ranch Christmas tree lighting. I've been here every single year, but I've never stood by her side as her other half and that means the world to me. We stand just off to the side, near her dad, with Joy and Ethan standing together on the other side hand in hand. Hope grins over at her sister, wearing all black, except for her cherry red shirt underneath her coat. She's standing close to Ethan, with his brown winter coat zipped up tight, glancing down at Joy, with admiration. Hope glances up at me, her happiness emanating off her as she steps a little closer to me. I stand behind her and rest my hands on her arms, hoping to keep both of us a little warmer. Then we both bring our focus back to her dad. He's wearing a black knit hat, pulled down over his ears and his familiar red and black plaid, wool-lined winter coat.

Frank turns and smiles at us and then at Joy and Ethan, appearing more content than I've seen him in a very long time. Then he turns and takes a few steps forward, fighting his limp in the cold, while he prepares to say a few words. He picks up the switch to light the Christmas tree and steps back towards us, before turning around to address the crowd. He clears his throat and holds his hands out as he calls out, "Thank you everyone for coming tonight! Thank you," he repeats. Then he waits momentarily for everyone to settle down. A hush comes over the crowd and everyone directs their attention to Frank. "This has been a terrific year for Evergreen Valley, for Two Sisters Ranch, not to mention the McGregor family," he begins, his voice heard clearly throughout the crowd. He takes a deep breath before he continues. "As many of you may or may not know, my daughter, Hope, is engaged to Gabriel Corsetti," he proudly announces. Everyone claps and cheers at his statement, while Hope glances up at me with a wide smile. I grin down at her, giving her shoulders a light squeeze to emphasize the overwhelming feeling of love and peace that washes over me. When it becomes quiet again, I tear my gaze away from her and attempt to pay attention to Frank's speech. He turns around and looks at me and takes a deep breath. Then he requests, "Gabe, why don't you come up here, please?"

My eyes widen in surprise and I gesture to myself. "Me?" I question.

Frank nods his head in confirmation and with smiling eyes, he confirms, "Yeah."

I let my hands slide down Hope's arms, reluctantly releasing her as she nudges me with her elbow urging me forward. I look at her with a question in my eyes, not quite sure where this is going. She grins up at me, her eyes sparkling and giving me a sense of comfort. She nods her head towards her dad and encourages, "Go, ahead." I give her a nod in acceptance and notice a knowing exchange pass between her and Joy, before I reluctantly leave her side. I take a step towards Frank, with no idea what to expect.

He puts his hand on my shoulder as a sign of support. "Gabe," he starts, "Two Sisters Ranch has been doing this tree lighting ceremony for fifty-five years. When I got engaged to my Gracey, her father passed the switch on to me. He told me that I brought a new light to his family. I never really knew what that meant until now," he explains. He pauses and clears his throat, the emotion of the moment obviously getting to him, causing me to choke up as well. He looks me in the eyes and continues, "You have brought a brighter light to this family than I ever did." I shake my head, slightly, not believing that could be true. Frank is an amazing man. "You have reignited a spark for a flame we thought went out five years ago," he states. My stomach twists and I take a steadying breath. I quickly glance at Hope for her reaction. I need to make sure she's okay, but she's still smiling happily at me. I gulp down the lump in my throat and look back at Frank as he resumes. "It's only right that you do the honors and light the tree tonight," he announces. Then he holds out the switch to me.

I gasp, as my mouth drops slightly open. I shake my head lightly in disbelief. Frank is the only one I've ever seen light the tree. Sometimes he's hit the switch with the help of his wife or daughters, but he's always been there. I take a deep breath and a smile tugs at my lips as I realize what an honor this is and it's completely unexpected. I look him in the eyes and murmur my appreciation, "Wow. Thanks, Frank." I glance back at Hope and she's grinning from ear to ear. She puts her hand to her mouth and then blows me a kiss, making me tingle on both the inside and out. I feel my face heat and I grin back at Hope, overwhelmed with the emotion that I'm now truly a part of this family, of Hope's family.

"Ready?" Frank prompts, interrupting our moment.

Instead of answering him right away, I walk over to Hope and reach for her hand. She smiles up at me as I entwine our fingers together. I look down at her and grin wide, trying to let her see in my eyes how deep she's ingrained in my heart and soul. I give her hand a gentle tug, taking her back with me to the tree and her dad. I turn back to him, a proud smile lighting up my face, now that I'm ready to answer his question with Hope by my side. I give him a firm nod and confidently declare, "Ready." He grins and I glance lovingly down at Hope, wondering if either of them realize my declaration means so much more than lighting up the Christmas tree. When I think about everything he just voiced to practically the whole town, I have to believe he understands what this means to me. I am incredibly honored to have this family tradition passed on to me; I just see it as a symbol for so much more. Then again, I don't think I'm the only one. I pick up the switch and hold it along with Hope, as we await her father's countdown.

"One," Frank begins counting, aloud. "Two," he continues, pausing after each number. "Three!" he loudly declares.

Hope and I flip the switch in our hands, instantly activating the lights on the Christmas tree and all the lights around the corral at the same time. Cheers erupt all around us, as everyone regards all the lights and decorations with awe, even if it's not a 40-foot tree.

We set the switch down and Hope lets go of my hand to wrap her arm around my waist. I lift my arm and drape it over her shoulders. I pull her close to me, while we all look up admiring the tree. "It really is beautiful, Gabe," Hope whispers. "Thank you," she adds.

I look down at her, thankful to have her in my arms, as the colorful lights of the Christmas tree, dance across her face and mine. "The tree doesn't matter, Hope," I insist. "As long as we're together," I confess.

She grins in response as a wistful sigh escapes through her parted lips. "I agree, Gabe," she happily concurs.

"I love you, Hope," I murmur, confidently. I feel as if my heart is overflowing with my love for this woman, but each moment, I find I love her more. How is that even possible?

"I love you, too, Gabe," she rasps. My heartbeat begins to race at her words. I lean towards her and kiss her on the corner of her mouth, holding her close. I don't think I could ever hear those words come out of her mouth enough.

I take her by the hand, entwining our fingers together. I pull it up to my lips and kiss the back of it, before we walk over and join the rest of the crowd. Joy strides over to us holding two steaming cups of their homemade hot chocolate. She smiles as she hands them to us. "Here, you two enjoy," she offers.

Hope's eyes widen and she exclaims, "Oh, I'm sorry Joy! I wasn't thinking about the hot chocolate," she declares. "I'll help you," she adds. She releases my hand and takes a step towards her sister.

Joy puts her hand out to stop her. "Not this time. You always do so much around here. Enjoy tonight with your fiancé," she emphasizes.

"We are enjoying ourselves," Hope insists. "We can both help with the hot chocolate," she suggests, with a quick glance in my direction.

"I'm sure that's exactly what Gabe wants to do," Joy mutters.

"If you want me to help, I will," I tell Hope.

"Why don't you take these two hot chocolates and bring them over to your mom and dad," Hope suggests. "That will give you a few minutes to talk to them before they leave," she adds.

I nod in agreement, "Okay."

"I'll help Joy with the rest," she adds. "There's too many people here for you to do this all by yourself," she proclaims.

"Thanks, Hope," Joy says, relenting.

Hope hands me the other cup, her fingers brushing mine as I take it from her. She pushes up on her tiptoes, placing a sweet kiss on my cheek. I smile down at her, my heart skipping a beat. Like I said before, it's the simple things that mean everything to me.

Chapter 25

Joy

Hope and I continue handing out cups of our special hot chocolate to all the guests gathered around the Christmas tree. As we make our way around outside, we can't help getting caught up in conversations with everyone as we go. I smile at my dad as I walk by him, returning to the full tray of hot chocolate I just brought outside. "Where's mine?" dad inquires, stopping me before I get there. Then he chuckles softly to let me know he's kidding.

I giggle and roll my eyes dramatically, pretending to be annoyed. Then I turn around and take the two steps towards the table set up off to the side, where I placed the tray. I carefully reach for another steaming mug of hot chocolate, automatically inhaling the sweet smell. I turn back to my dad and close the distance between us. I grin proudly as I hand him the cup. "I would never forget you, Dad," I insist.

He smiles appreciatively, "Thank you, Sweetheart." He takes a small sip and moans in appreciation. "I know neither of you girls would forget me, but we all know this hot chocolate is one of the reasons our neighbors would never even think of missing a tree lighting," he reminds me. The corners of his mouth twitch upwards in delight. He loves having everyone here, enjoying the ranch and spending time together. He's always so busy worrying about Hope or me and working so hard. It's really nice to see him relishing his time relaxing, as well as laughing and chatting with friends and family. He doesn't do it nearly often enough. Plus, I'm sure Hope and Gabe's engagement has made this year's tree lighting all the more special for him. I know it has for me and without a doubt it has for both of them.

Mr. Wendt, a friend of my dad's from down the road steps up next to us, chuckling. "He's right, you know," he declares, gesturing towards my dad. He's a big man like my dad, tall and broad, with a full head of gray hair, blue eyes, and a square jaw.

Dad's grin grows wider and I hold up my finger in mock warning, "Hey don't go giving him any ideas. He already thinks he's always right."

They both laugh in response. My dad puts his free arm around me and pulls me close to him, kissing me on the top of the head. "Thanks, Joy."

"This truly is the best hot chocolate," Mr. Wendt claims. "I look forward to it every year," he adds reverently.

"Thank you," I murmur, appreciatively. "I think our biggest concern is usually if we'll have enough for everyone," I admit.

"I believe it," he concedes.

I smile politely and take a step back, as dad and Mr. Wendt begin talking about the new restaurant in town, like so many others. I look around the crowd, searching for Ethan, but I don't see him anywhere. I glance back at my dad and wait for a moment to interrupt. "Dad, have you seen Ethan?" I inquire.

He nods his head in confirmation. "Yes, I believe he went back to the inn when you and Hope went inside to get more hot chocolate for the guests," he informs me, gesturing towards the back door of the inn. "At least he

209

was headed in that direction the last time I saw him," he adds.

I nod my head in acknowledgement. "Okay, thanks," I murmur. I bite my lower lip and take a step back, debating if I should stay here, or if I could get away to go check on Ethan. I glance longingly in the direction of the inn.

Dad chuckles softly and grins. He nods his head in the direction of the inn and encourages me to go find him. "Go ahead, Joy."

"Thanks, Dad," I mumble, gratefully. A smile tugs at my lips as I begin bouncing on my toes. I push up on my tiptoes and give my dad a kiss on the cheek; loving the adoring look he gives me in response. Then I spin on my heel, and stride back towards the inn. I quickly weave my way through the crowd, hoping nobody tries to stop me on the way. I step inside the door near the kitchen and slip my coat off as I walk towards the front office. I go inside and hang my coat on one of the hooks inside the back closet. Then I make my way back to the kitchen and look for another colorful Christmas mug. I find a red one wrapped with green and white Christmas stockings and reach for it. I pour a steaming cup of hot chocolate out of the giant carafe. Then I pick it up and cautiously walk towards Ethan's room. I want to be careful not to spill any on the way, but mostly it's so I don't have to stop to clean it up right away.

I step up to his door and pause, biting my lower lip in hesitation. I don't want to interrupt his writing or anything else, but he didn't even say goodbye before he took off tonight. I sigh and smile to myself, anxious to see him. Besides, I don't want him to miss out on our famous hot chocolate either, so I'm actually doing him a huge favor by coming up here, at least that's what I'm going to tell myself. I take a deep breath and square my shoulders.

Then I release my lip, with renewed confidence. I mumble to myself, "Hopefully, he'll like this surprise." I hold my free hand up and knock on the door, before I have a chance to change my mind again. My heart begins to pound erratically, as I anxiously wait for him to answer.

I hear the sound of Ethan's footsteps approaching, just before he pulls the door open. His eyes widen in surprise as he meets my gaze, followed by a slow, easy smile. His pearly white smile against his tanned skin is quickly becoming the cause of me nearly melting into a puddle at his feet. It literally takes my breath away every single time. "Hi," he greets me.

"Hi," I respond, simply. I grin up at him from underneath my long lashes, happy to see him, as if it's been days, instead of only minutes. Then I take a step forward, holding the mug of hot chocolate out to him. "Here, this is for you," I announce.

He grins as he reaches for the cup. His fingers softly brush mine, as he happily accepts the mug, sending goosebumps traveling up my arms like lightning and quickly spreading throughout the rest of my body. I watch as he pulls the cup up to his face, tipping his nose towards the creamy, sweet, brown liquid. He closes his eyes and inhales deeply. A grateful smile instantly lights up his face, as if the smell alone brings back special memories. "Hot chocolate," he mumbles, groaning in appreciation. He slowly opens his eyes and meets my gaze. "My favorite," he enlightens me, his voice a quiet rumble.

I feel my insides instantly warm, happy I was able to do something for him, even if it seems simple. I know better than anyone that all the little things make a huge difference. The little things and the people you're with are the things that make memories so special. "Not just any hot chocolate," I declare, proudly. "My sister's famous hot chocolate," I emphasize. "We passed it out after the tree lighting," I explain, "but you disappeared," I claim. I press my lips tightly together, in attempt to hide my disappointment.

He nods his head in acknowledgement, appearing a little bit regretful. "I felt inspired and I needed to write," he explains.

I nod my head in understanding, while internally I breathe a sigh of relief. "I get it," I confess, honestly. I used to have that same feeling all the time when I was writing more often. I still do, but my writing has gotten put on hold a lot more often since the accident, whether I have that feeling or not. I'm usually setting writing aside to do something else that needs to be done, either at the inn or around the ranch. My family has had to be my priority, but it was my choice to make it that way. I don't regret it. My family has always been the most important thing in the world to me and I would never change that.

Ethan cradles the cup in his hands and leans casually against the doorway, crossing his feet at his ankles. He looks at me with curiosity filling his gaze. "Gabe told me you were a writer too," he informs me.

My eyes widen in astonishment, since I hadn't yet shared that part of me with Ethan. I quickly shake off my shock and confirm, "I still am." I may not write as much as I used to, but it will always be a part of me. Plus, I believe there will be a time when writing will be my focus again. "I've got notebooks hidden all over the house," I confess, surprising myself.

He grins and a look of understanding crosses over his face. "Maybe you can show me some of your writing sometime?" he requests, his expression hopeful.

My heartbeat speeds up and I take a slow, deep breath, trying to calm my anxiety at the mere thought of him reading some of my writing. It's scary for someone to see so much of what you hold deep inside you, no matter what type of writing it may be. Then again, Hope is the only one that I've really let read some of my stuff, besides my professors. Ethan is the first person, I think I want to consider sharing it with outside of my family and school. "Maybe," I reply. I shrug my shoulders as if it's no big deal, but it definitely is a big deal to me. "Speaking of writing," I begin, attempting to change the subject, "how's the novel coming?"

He nods his head, as the corners of his mouth curve up in another smile. He responds confidently and exclaims, "Great! I'm almost done," he proclaims.

I gasp, my mouth dropping open in shock. "Really?" I question. "A novel in a week?" I prompt, arching my eyebrows in challenge. How does someone even write that fast? Does he ever get a chance to sleep? His rough draft is really almost done?

He grins and nods his head in confirmation. "You'd be surprised what I can do when I'm inspired," he asserts. His hazel eyes sparkle brightly as he looks at me, causing my stomach to flip-flop and prompt my curiosity.

I shove my questions to the back of my mind, hoping we'll have more time to talk about it later. I tilt my head up towards him and give him a sly smile. "Maybe, one day, I'll find out," I respond, challenging him.

He chuckles softly at my bold statement. The soft sound rumbles right through me and makes my breath momentarily catch in my throat. I quickly gulp it down as I wait for his reply. "Maybe," he answers, giving me a crooked smile.

I take a deep breath, reminding myself it's probably time for me to leave. I did interrupt his work and he has a deadline. "Get back to your writing, Mr. Dulane," I encourage, smiling up at him. "I'll see you tomorrow," I reiterate. I really like the sound of those words. I'd love to see a lot more of Mr. Dulane.

I spin on my heel and stride back down the hallway, knowing he's watching me walk away. "Good night," he calls after me. I smile to myself and keep walking, not allowing myself to look back. It has been a really long time since any man has given me butterflies like that and with Ethan, it feels like there's a whole swarm of them ready to take over all my insides. I make my way back downstairs and into the kitchen to help cleanup.

I cross my arms over my chest and glance outside, noticing several people still milling around the Christmas tree. I sigh and lean against the counter, thinking about what Ethan said about my writing. I don't know if I'm ready to share my writing, it's so personal. Plus, my writing is nothing like his. Writing romance has just never been one of my strengths. But as a writer, I think you learn to appreciate all different styles. Maybe he would like what I write. I think if I decide to share my writing with anyone, it's going to be Ethan. I guess it can't hurt to look through some of my stuff and see if I can find something I'd be ready and willing to share with him. And maybe I'm ready to show him more than I think.

I push off the counter and walk back to the front office to grab my coat. I should probably go back outside. I'm sure they'll need my help picking up all the cups out there and there's really not a lot of places we can leave them outside.

Chapter 26

Hope

I tighten Westie's cinch and then double-check the stirrups and the reigns. I reach up and run my hand lovingly down his neck. "What do you think Westie?" I ask the horse, grinning. "Do you want to go for a ride?" I question, as if he'll answer me back.

I laugh softly at myself, but I can't help it. I'm really excited to go riding again. It almost feels like I'm about to go riding for the first time. I'm a little nervous, but I think that's because I don't want anyone to make a big deal out of it. I just finally feel like I'm ready. I've been sleeping well again and I feel at peace when memories of my mom and Aunt come about. I also think part of it, is knowing I have Gabe's support no matter what I choose to do. I've always had my family and Gabe has always been there for me, but something inside me feels different having him backing me with his whole heart and soul. I unclip Westie, grasping his lead in my hand. Then I give him one more adoring pat along his side and guide him to come along with me. "Come on, let's go, Westie," I softly call out. Then I turn and make my way out of the barn.

"Hey, Hope!" Joy exclaims, as she approaches me.

"Morning!" I greet her, smiling wide.

Joy's eyebrows draw down in confusion as she looks at Westie and then back to me. I bite my lip, trying not to laugh, knowing exactly what she's thinking. "Where's Westie going?" she finally inquires. "There aren't any trail rides scheduled until noon," she vocalizes, as her way of asking if there's something she doesn't know.

I shrug and concede, "I know. I was thinking of taking him out myself," I admit, a smile tugging at my lips. I glance up at her to see her reaction.

Her eyes widen in surprise and she audibly gasps. "Really?" she prompts, her eyes brighten instantly.

I pat Westie, looking up at him, adoringly. Then I nod my head in confirmation. "Yeah. I've missed him," I confess. "It's about time," I acknowledge. "Don't you think?" I question. I look at her, no longer fighting the smirk that wants to break through.

Joy breaks out into a broad smile, her whole face lighting up. She practically shakes with excitement as she requests, "Can I come?"

I breathe a sigh of relief and grin as I nod my head in agreement. "Sure. Kaya is ready," I inform her, gesturing towards the stables. I got her ready earlier in case Joy wanted to join me, but I didn't want to go looking for her to announce my plan either, nervous I might change my mind if there was too much talking about it. I'm just really glad she found me.

"Be right back!" she replies, her excitement contagious. I laugh as I watch her jog quickly towards the stables, as if I might leave without her if she doesn't hurry.

I continue to pat Westie's side, as I watch her go. "What do you think Westie?" I prod. He neighs, happily as if he knows what's happening. Then again, maybe he does. I have always thought of him as my horse with our strong connection.

Gabe

I turn around and find Joy escorting Kaya out of her stable, ready for a ride. "Do you have a trail ride this morning, Joy?" I question. I don't remember seeing anything on the schedule, but things pop up last minute all the time.

Joy turns and looks at me, with Kaya's lead in her hand. She's grinning from ear to ear and bouncing on her toes, barely able to contain her excitement. She shakes her head and responds, "Nope! I'm just going riding," she announces, a mischievous sparkle in her eyes.

My eyebrows draw down in confusion, knowing I haven't seen her this excited to go riding since she was a little girl. My heartbeat speeds up and I take a small step towards her feeling the anticipation radiating off of her. I gulp down a rising lump in my throat and prompt, "What's going on Joy? What aren't you telling me?"

She laughs softly and glances outside, as if she doesn't want anyone to overhear us. Then she faces me and proudly, but quietly informs me, "I'm going riding with Hope."

My heart skips a beat and I gasp, as my mouth drops open in shock. "With Hope?" I repeat, as if I didn't hear her right. She nods her head in confirmation. "With my Hope?" I reiterate, needing the clarification.

"Yup!" she announces, giggling, with a smug look on her face.

"Well, get out of here then," I encourage, waving her away. "Go!" I prompt, wanting to push her out the door. She throws her head back and laughs as she turns and strides out of the stable, leading Kaya outside.

I carefully make my way over to the edge of the barn doorway, afraid if I make too much noise, it could draw Hope's attention. If I know her at all, I know she doesn't want anyone to make a big deal out of this. It's probably the reason she didn't tell anyone. She definitely won't want me watching her, but there's no way I'm going to miss this moment. I just don't need her to know I'm watching until after she's back. I carefully peek around the corner and spot Joy approaching Hope and Westie.

"Morning, Gabe," Ethan's voice comes from behind me, startling me and nearly blowing my cover.

I quickly quiet him, "Shhh," and wave him behind me. He steps behind me before he crouches over and peers around the entryway in attempt to see what I'm looking it. I watch Hope for any kind of reaction, but she doesn't even spare a glance in my direction. I quietly breathe a sigh of relief and continue to stare after her.

"What are you doing?" he whispers.

"I think Hope is going to ride," I answer, without looking at him.

"Really?" he asks.

I nod my head in confirmation, "Yeah. She hasn't ridden since," I begin.

Ethan interrupts, completing my thoughts. "Her mom died. Yeah, Joy told me," Ethan reveals, his voice full of empathy.

"I don't want to distract her," I explain. "This is a pretty big moment," I proclaim, my heart clenching with love and pride for her.

Ethan reaches into his pocket and pulls out his phone. He holds it out and aims it towards Joy and Hope.

"What are you doing?" I prompt.

He grins and acknowledges, "Someday, she'll want a picture of this."

I grin wider and nod at him in appreciation. "Good call," I declare. Then I turn my focus back to Hope, not wanting to miss anything.

I hear Joy gleefully announce, "Let's saddle up!"

Hope nods and pulls herself up onto Westie's back. Then she takes a minute to readjust herself in the saddle and the reigns in her hands. A look of contentment and happiness passes over her face, causing my chest to ache with love and pride. Then, she takes off in the direction of the trails, with Joy right at her side.

It's amazing to see her on a horse again. It's the way it should be. I smile at the sight of Hope and Joy riding out towards the trails, side by side, just like they used to do when they were kids. It's an absolutely beautiful sight. The sun shines through the trees, glimmering down on them. It feels like it's their mom and Aunt smiling down on them. I gulp down the lump in my throat as my chest tightens again. My love for Hope practically overwhelms me as they disappear into the trees. Her strength and resilience are awe-inspiring. Every time I think I couldn't be more in love with her, she does something to prove me wrong. I love it when she proves me wrong. I feel like the luckiest man in the world.

Ethan chuckles softly. I turn around and look back at him, my eyebrows drawn down in question. "What?" I prompt.

He points to the small, framed picture on the wall of the barn and informs me, "It's almost the same view, but now they're all grown-up."

I walk over to the picture and huff a laugh as I look at the image. It's a picture from behind and a little off to the side of Joy and Hope on horseback, heading out to the trails. "They were probably eleven or twelve years old in this picture," I mumble. Hope's beautiful, brown curls are pulled back in a short ponytail and she's wearing a faded jean jacket, similar to the one she wears now, along with jeans and dark brown riding boots. Joy's long, blonde hair hangs straight underneath her straw cowboy hat, with a dark blue jean jacket, a stylish pink and white flannel hanging out underneath, dark blue jeans and brown cowboy boots with elaborate pink stitching. I chuckle at the similarities to the women they've become.

Ethan holds his phone up by the picture, the photo he just took lighting up his screen. Hope has her curly hair up in a ponytail, while Joy's hair is smooth hanging out from underneath her cowboy hat. Even their clothes are similar with their jeans, jean jackets, Hope's simple brown cowboy boots and Joy's brown with intricate teal stitching, Hope's simple teal green sweater underneath and Joy's stylish cream sweater under hers. "Wow," he murmurs.

I nod in acknowledgement. It's a little bit surreal looking at the photos side by side. "It's almost the exact same picture," I confirm. Hope and Joy will love that," I insist, feeling my own emotions overwhelming me. He smiles in satisfaction and I nod in acknowledgement before I turn away. I glance out in the direction they just rode towards and a smile tugs at my lips, a feeling of peace washing over me. I feel like things are finally as they should be.

Joy

Hope leads the way as we enter the trails through a break in the trees. I follow her into the woods as we pick up one of the trails. We hear the clopping of our horses' hooves and the crunch of fallen leaves underfoot, as we approach a break in the path, although most leaves have been cleared into the brush along the sides. I take a deep breath, the smell of snow in the air.

I'm thrilled to be riding with Hope again. I never stopped riding, but I missed the time we used to spend together on horseback. It was always different when we would ride together. We spend the time enjoying the horses and scenery, but mostly talking and laughing like I can only do with her. It's been way too long. I'm so proud of her, I can barely contain my excitement.

She pauses and glances back in my direction. "Where do you think you want to ride to?" Hope inquires.

"I think it's your turn to lead the way," I prompt. "I'll go wherever you want to go today and however long you want to ride for," I admit.

She giggles and declares, "I like the sound of that."

"Don't go getting any ideas," I playfully warn her. "I'm just talking about this particular ride," I tease.

She laughs and insists, "You got it, Joy." She pauses and quietly adds, "Thanks for coming with me."

I open my mouth to respond, but Hope doesn't give me the chance. She suddenly digs her heels in and makes a clicking sound twice with her mouth, prompting Westie to take off in a fast trot, down the trail. I laugh and follow behind her, enjoying the scenery and the time with my sister. The sun shines down through the trees, illuminating our surroundings. I tilt my face upwards to feel the warmth on my face, feeling as if mom and Aunt Faith are here with us and smiling. I don't think today could be any better. It feels as if things are finally as they should be. I grin and click my tongue two times, urging Kaya to catch up with Hope and Westie.

Epilogue

One Year Later...

Ethan

I'm sitting outside at a small, wrought iron bistro table, bundled up in jeans, a thick, olive green, lined sweatshirt, with two rounded brown buttons at the top and my comfortable and warm brown winter coat. A dwindling stack of my new book, "Joy & Hope" sits in front of me. On the cover is the same picture of Joy and Hope I found in the barn last year of the two of them riding together when they were kids, with the snow just starting to fall all around them. It's also the same picture they replicated nearly a year ago. I reach for a book, grabbing one off the top of the pile. Then I open the cover and sign a short greeting just inside, before I sign my name. Then, I close the book and hold it out to my waiting fan. She has short grey hair, matching eyes and a friendly smile. "Thank you," she states, politely.

"Merry Christmas," I reply, offering her a smile, as she happily accepts the book from my hands. She grins in response and waves, just before she turns and walks away.

A young teen fan, with long blonde hair and bright blue eyes steps up to the table right behind her. She's wearing a Christmas red winter dress coat. She smiles brightly as I take one of the last books in the pile and sign it for her. I hand it to her and she hugs it tightly to her chest, giving me a smile so big it's contagious. "Thank you, Mr. Dulane. Merry Christmas," she happily proclaims.

"Merry Christmas," I respond. Then she turns and strides towards her family, a bounce of excitement in her steps.

Joy sidles up beside me, placing her hand on my shoulder, displaying her 2-carat diamond and platinum engagement ring, as she kisses me on the cheek. I lean back in my chair and glance up at her, warmth spreading throughout my body at the sight of her bright smile. She looks incredibly beautiful in black jeans, a soft gray sweater with a lacey design up by her neck, black cowboy boots and a black winter coat hanging down to her knees. She brushes her hair back with her free hand, as it falls over her shoulders in loose curls. I can't help, but smile up at her. "Some hot chocolate for you, Mr. Dulane," she announces. I tear my gaze away from hers and bring my attention to the cup of hot chocolate I didn't realize she was holding out for me.

"Why, thank you, soon-to-be Mrs. Dulane," I reply, a wide grin on my face. She leans a little closer and brushes her lips softly against mine. The gesture gives me chills down my spine, just like the first time I kissed her. She lowers herself onto my knee and my arm automatically wraps around her petite waist.

"I love the sound of that," she murmurs, as she looks into my eyes, her blue eyes sparkling. I grin up at her, knowing exactly what she means. I feel the same way.

Hope saunters up to us, her pregnant belly showing, under her blue-green turtleneck and long, grey, wool vest. "Come on, you two," she encourages. "It's time for the tree lighting," she announces, resting her hand gently on her belly.

"Okay, thanks Hope," I acknowledge, with a quick glance in her direction.

"We're coming," Joy declares.

I take a sip of my hot chocolate and set it down on the table, knowing I'll need both hands for the tree lighting this year. Joy leans down and gives me another sweet kiss on the corner of my mouth before she slips off my lap and stands up. She grabs my hands and lightly tugs, like she has to urge me to come with her, but I'll always follow her wherever she goes. I stand up and immediately clasp her hand in mine, as I look down on her with love and respect. We slowly make our way over to the Christmas tree, just as Hope rejoins Gabe in front of the tree. He instinctively lets one hand immediately fall protectively over her belly, while the other rests on her shoulder, her back to his chest.

We watch as the growing crowd of friends, family, neighbors and guests begin to settle around the large forty foot Christmas tree. Gabe did an amazing job making the Christmas tree look fantastic last year, but a tree like this is really something to see. Now, I understand what all the fuss was about last year, but last Christmas still turned into an amazing one, even without the forty-foot tree.

"It's your turn this year," she whispers, reminding me.

"I'm ready," I insist. And I believe I am ready. I'm ready to be a part of everything about her, including her family traditions. I stand next to Joy, my hands resting gently on her shoulders, as Frank steps in front of the crowd of family, friends and guests to give his annual speech.

He holds out his arms and easily quiets everyone down. He takes a deep breath and begins, "Thank you everyone for coming tonight. We've had another wonderful year here at the ranch and with our family. I know my Gracey is looking down on all of us and smiling. We have our first grandchild on the way," he announces. Then he pauses as applause breaks out all around. He glances back at Gabe and Hope with pride and love, as they both grin with pure happiness and rosy cheeks. Then he turns back to the crowd and proclaims, "And those of you who don't know Ethan Dulane," he pauses and gestures towards me. I smile and nod my head in response, before he continues. "He was a guest here at the ranch last year at this time. He was here to find some inspiration for his book that was released in February, "No Mistletoe," he pauses again for the erupting cheers. "But he found a lot more than just a little inspiration with my Joy. Joy and Ethan are engaged and it's time to welcome him into the family," he proudly announces, grinning wide. Applause breaks out all around us. He glances in our direction and requests, "Ethan, will you join me up here?"

"Absolutely," I declare, with complete confidence. I give Joy's shoulders a gentle squeeze and slide my hand down her arm, clasping her hand in mine. I smile down at her and my heart skips a beat at her answering grin. Then we walk together, hand in hand, up to her dad. He's wearing a white and cherry red flannel shirt, with dark blue jeans, a short, black dress coat and a black beanie hat atop his head.

"Ethan," Frank begins, "the day you arrived on the ranch marks the same time there was a big turning point in this family, a wonderful turning point. We're all happy you and Joy found each other and that you decided to stay." Joy gives my hand a squeeze at this comment, broadening my smile. I wouldn't want to be anywhere else. "It's time to welcome you into the McGregor family by giving you the opportunity to light the tree this year for our family."

"Thank you," I tell him, appreciatively. I momentarily slip my hand away from Joy's and hold my hand out to her dad. He shakes it, at the same time pulling me in for a quick one-armed hug. He releases me and I immediately hold my hand out for Joy. She slides her hand in mine and we step over to the switch together. I look down at her with a broad smile on my face, admittedly a little overwhelmed with emotion. I'm thrilled to be a part of this family tradition and soon to be part of this family. It feels as if this chapter of our lives is ending in the same place it all began. At the same time, a new one is just beginning. More than anything, I can't wait to discover what the next chapter holds for all of us.

"Ready?" Frank inquires.

I give him a firm nod of my head and proclaim, "Ready."

He smiles at both Joy and me as he begins to count loud and slow, pausing between each number for emphasis, "One, Two, Three!"

We flip the switch and the crowd erupts in cheers. I look down at Joy with a wide grin and she immediately loops her arms around my neck. I lower my lips to hers without hesitation and kiss her sweetly. I pull back and smile down at her as I swing her around, enjoying the light sound of her laughter, before I gently set her back on her feet. She sighs happily and turns around, facing the tree, while my arms engulf her from behind. She lets her head fall back on my shoulder, as we both look up, admiring the lights and the tree, along with all the meaning behind it for both of us. "I love you, Ethan

Dulane," she whispers, happily, as she stares up at the tree.

I smile down at her and gently place a kiss on the top of her head. "I love you too, Joy," I murmur, feeling as if my heart is truly full. I never imagined that when I was sent to Two Sisters ranch, I would not only find my inspiration for my next book, but also my inspiration for my future and the love of my life. I'm exactly where I'm supposed to be.

The End

Acknowledgements

I would like to take this opportunity to thank everyone who has helped with this book. First, I would like to thank Douglas C. Diana for investing in this Christmas movie. Without you, the movie or the book would never have come to be. Thank you to Amy Minter, Producer of the film for your constant support! I, of course, need to thank my good friend, Candy Cain for asking me to collaborate with you once again on this Christmas movie (and book) project. Between set, breakfasts and wandering around my backyard while talking out different directions of this story, I really enjoyed working with you! Watching everything come together for the movie and the book was incomparable. Thank you for asking me to be a part of this wonderful adventure.

I would like to thank Cody Calafiore, Ashley Brinkman, Andrew Rogers, Alix Kermes, Stink Fisher, Vivica A Fox and the rest of the cast who helped bring these wonderful characters to life in the film and on the pages. I really enjoyed working with everyone in the cast and crew and I loved seeing the film for the first time on screen. I love being able to tell stories in all these different ways. Thank you to the O'Toole family who were all incredibly gracious throughout filming in their beautiful home and working with all their gorgeous horses. It was truly the perfect setting for this story and the animals were amazing!

Thank you to Marisol Farrell for taking some beautiful pictures of young Joy and Hope with the horses, as well as the young actresses who portray them and to Veronica Grella for turning those pictures into art for the cover. Thank you to Graphic Designer, Constantine Chutis, for designing the book cover quickly to use as a prop during filming and for the actual paperback and e-book covers. All of you did remarkable work!

Thank you to Kelley and Nancy for all that you do and to all of my Beta Readers. I greatly appreciate all of your input and reviews. I value each and every one of you. Thank you, most of all, to my friends and family for their continuous support. I wouldn't be here without ALL of you. I love you all! And no matter what time of year it is when you read this, Merry Christmas!

I need to do a separate special thank you to Andrew Rogers who plays character Ethan Dulane and "writer" of this book. This made the project even more unique, which I love. It challenged me in my writing to write as the male character writing his adventure romance novel. Now, who knows, maybe you'll be seeing more of Ethan Dulane. Of course, this puts his face on the back of your book covers. Plus, I thought I'd also share this from set of Andrew and myself (author and character author) with one of the beautiful horses.

For more Family Contemporary Romance, read more by Nicole Mullaney and Ethan Dulane. Connect with Nicole here:

Follow Me on Instagram
@nicolemullaney

For Adult Contemporary Romance, read books by Nikki A Lamers. Connect with her here:

Official Author Website
www.nikkialamersauthor.com

Author Facebook Page
www.facebook.com/pg/NikkiALamersAuthor

Follow Me on Instagram
@NikkialamersAuthor

Author Goodreads Page
www.goodreads.com/author/show/8451774.Nikki_A_La
mers

Amazon Author Page
https://www.amazon.com/Nikki-A.-
Lamers/e/B00NU1VU8M

For more information on Gemelli Films, find them here:

Official Website
http://Gemellifilm.com/

Gemelli Films Facebook Page
https://m.facebook.com/GemelliFilms/

Follow #gemellifilms on Instagram